SPARK

ISBN-13: 978-0692176450
ISBN-10: 0692176454

I don't know where I am, but I know it's a bathroom. I'm sitting on tile with my head resting against a toilet. It's a stall, the plastic door and the broken lock. I can hear people—the stomp stomp of their shoes and the clack of their heels and the running of their water. There's an announcer announcing something far off in the distance. I must be at the goddamned Port Authority.

I'm wet all over from definitely piss and probably beer. The back of my pants are soaked, and the front of my shirt reeks of vomit. Fucking Christa was supposed to take me home.

I stand up. The tile is cold but only on my right foot. I'm missing a shoe evidently. My head is like a thousand fires burning on top of each other. Fires. I get a chill because I'm thinking about fire again. Back when—way back when—I remember Sam telling me to calm down. "It's all I can think about," I said. It was true. I just kept seeing it. I still see it sometimes, but mostly in front of a joint or a pipe. I need to see Papi.

I walk out of the stall and a fucking Upper East bitch stops staring at herself in the mirror and stares at me.

"What's the matter," I say, my voice slurring and jilted—more than I thought it'd be, "you haven't partied before?"

She looks back at the mirror and I walk to the sink beside her and turn on the water. Hot. Steaming. I can tell she's uncomfortable. Uncomfortable just standing next to me. I'm not going to make another comment—I feel bad enough for the one already—and, looking at the mirror, she has every right to stare.

I look like shit. Absolute shit. My hair is crusted with vomit, its dyed pink streaks flecked with browns and greens. Christa was supposed to take me home.

I walk out of the bathroom. It's Port Authority alright. The loud-speaking voices, the crowds. I look in through the front window of a pharmacy at a digital clock they have hung up on the wall. It's 1:34 in the afternoon. No sense even trying to get to work today. I check my purse—somehow I still have it—and pull out my wallet. I have a $10 bill which is just enough to get something to eat. I remember I'm starving, and I remember that was why I went into Port Authority in the first place. I wanted a slice of pizza.

As I walk through the terminal looking for a pizza place I get a big whiff of myself and lose my appetite. I need to calm down. It's coming again— that dark cloud, seeping through the walls and the cracks, searching, sliding down the escalators, carried on a foul wind that comes coughing out of the exhaust pipes from the busses upstairs, groping for me. My stomach begins to churn. The $10 is going to go to cigarettes instead. I need to calm down. I buy some from the pharmacy. I don't look at the cashier.

On a bench outside, I smoke while the heat and the water meld together in the thick air. The humidity is bringing out the smell more, but hopefully the cigarette will mask it—even just a little. No one looks at me and, if they do, it's only in short bursts. They seem embarrassed. I'm not embarrassed—not really. Maybe I should be.

Walking across the street, I descend down into the subway station and head south. The train's squealing does a number on my head and drowns out the loud hip-hop music that's blaring from the phone of an elderly man sitting near the rear of the car. He bobs his head up and down up and down to the beat, but I can barely hear it. I only hear the squealing.

I get off at my stop and walk up the steps into the boiling sun and wet, lighting another cigarette. July is the worst month, followed closely behind by February—for different reasons, obviously.

Last February was when Dad called. It wasn't like him. We hadn't spoken. We hadn't spoken in years. He asked how I was doing and if Jim had talked to me. He hadn't, and I said he hadn't. Dad said that he was going to—no—he said that he was trying to. What the hell does trying to mean? You either are talking, will talk, or won't talk. Did his fingers become too big to hit the buttons on his phone all of a sudden? Trying to. He knows my number. It hasn't...

Why would Jim be trying now, though. He had years. Years to try. But now...

When I arrive at our building, I stamp my cigarette out on the ground and put my key in the door. It's a tricky lock. You have to fumble and jingle it until it catches. It always does, though, and usually when you are just about to give up and call the landlord. That's a step you take as a last resort—always. Peter Lester is a huge, fat man with a temper that can go from 0 to 1,000 in about half a second. He's probably on something. He has to be. It's that kind of place.

No mouse in the trap by the doorstop—this time. I think there's one there probably thirty or forty percent of the time. Jim would know. He'd have it down to a science, scribbled out in note books with ratios and fractions and multiplications running this way and that, all pointing to the most likely time a mouse's head could get squashed. He was like that with everything. He did it for fun. I'm smiling, I realize. Jim...

I climb the stairs to apartment 4B. Our apartment—mine and Chuck's. I put the key in the door. This one isn't tricky at all. It goes in solid, its teeth grinding against the pins as I turn and pull the bolt inside.

"You didn't fucking come home last night," Chuck says as soon as I walk in, his words slurring. He's already drunk. Maybe still drunk. He's wearing the same clothes he did yesterday.

"Neither did you," I respond, and he juts out his jaw like some kind of monkey at the zoo, scratching his head when the keeper replaces one of his toys.

"Aren't you supposed to be working?" he asks, crashing down onto the metal folding chair next to the card table. They're the only pieces of furniture we own, save for the mattress in the bedroom.

"Aren't you supposed to be getting a job?" I

spit. I don't mean to, but "getting" comes out with a large glob of saliva that runs down my chin.

He stands up and lifts the chair over his head like one of those wrestlers in that stupid show he used to watch before he broke the TV. He screams, and throws it down hard on the ground, the metal reverberating, humming with the force of the impact.

"You're such a fucking child," I say, and he storms out the door, slamming it behind him.

He had vomit running down his shirt, too.

Sam wouldn't let me do this to myself. She would have stopped it a long time ago—probably would have committed a few felonies in the process—put Chuck in the hospital. Chuck's pretty scrawny. She could have taken him. When Kevin and his friends got me drunk that night by the river she pulled me onto the bank half-naked and stumbling and didn't let any of them near me. She took me back to her parents' place—luckily they were out of town—to spend the night. She made breakfast and we watched stupid TV in our underwear all the next day. She wouldn't have let me get with Chuck. I shouldn't have let me get with Chuck.

I go into the bathroom and open the window to air out the smell of stale cigarettes and beer, taking off my clothes and throwing them in the corner with the rest of the dirty laundry. It's been piling up. I'll have to go down to the cleaner's soon. Chuck isn't going to.

I climb into the shower and let the water wash

over me warm and almost burning as the putridity drizzles away down the drain. There is a mental exercise I know. Taught to me by a man I hate. It goes, breathe in the good and exhale the bad. I do it. I breathe in the good, but it tastes like chlorine and water. As I breathe out the bad, it's just air. It's a fucking stupid exercise, but I always remember it because I used to do it whenever I took a shower. I guess I still do it.

I step out and grab some clothes from the clean clothes pile in the bedroom. It's opposite the dirty one. I put on a white blouse and jeans and pull up the mattress, knowing what I'll find there. Nothing. Of course nothing. I'd know if there was something. I would have known if there was something and it would have been used up in that instant. It would have been gone just as fast as I could have known. That's how it always is when we score some. It becomes lost.

Chuck has a syringe in a pile of socks, but I'm not doing that shit. Jim said he tried it once. Just the one time. Everyone did back home. He said it made his blood feel like fire while his body was a corpse. Like a body burning from the inside. Burning. I'm not going to touch heroin. Chuck can fuck with that stuff. I have my boundaries.

Papi won't sell to Chuck anymore—not after Chuck tried to raid his stash while he was in the bathroom. He'll sell to me, though. I don't have much, but I don't really know how much I have. I think it's around the $80 range. Might not be enough. It depends on if Papi is in a good mood or not.

I put on some fresh makeup.

Papi, of course, isn't his real name. It's what we all call him, though—we being the people who buy coke off him. I think he told me his real name once, but I don't remember it. It was one night while we were all partying—me and Chuck's friend and Papi. He looked real scared right after he said it—looked around all bug-eyed and panicked.

"Now, you can't tell a soul, you hear me?" he said.

No one had heard him. We had all missed it—his name, I mean. The music had been too loud and half of us were doped out of our minds anyway. He spent the rest of the night pacing back and forth, rubbing his hands and scratching the back of his head until a tiny bald patch formed behind his ear.

The next time I saw him he was fine, and he's been fine ever since, I think. I don't really know. We don't talk about anything.

I find him at his usual spot, a café down west called Jay's. He's sitting in the corner booth drinking black coffee.

"I don't have any," he says as soon as I sit down across from him. He's a big guy, with a thick black pony tail.

"What do you mean you don't have any?" I ask.

"They cut me off. I'm leaving tomorrow. Going upstate—to the country—to wait it out."

"Wait what out?"

He looks around nervously, and leans in close. "You think this shit just comes down in the summer rain?" he says through gritted teeth. "Colombia. That's where they get almost all of it, and there's a lot of shit going down there these days." He sighs and leans back in his seat. "My contacts had to downsize. I was laid off. At least they gave me a decent separation package. I'm taking that and getting out of town before I get mistaken for someone I'm not and get the book thrown at me."

I scoff. "Why the hell are you going upstate? There's nothing up there. It's a wasteland."

"It's quiet."

I can feel the itch coming. "How the hell am I supposed to get my shit now though, Papi? How the hell am I supposed to—"

"I had to sign a non-disclosure agreement. I can't say. No one's selling out this way—at least not in your price range." He takes a sip of his coffee. "Heroin's prices are good right now."

"I don't do that shit."

He finishes his coffee and gets up from the table. "Might be a good time to start."

"Where the hell are you going?" I ask.

He raises his eyebrows, smiles, and walks out the door.

I follow him. Of course I follow him, but at a distance so he can't tell. He lights up a cigarette as he walks and so do I, our smoke mingling up above people's heads somewhere. He walks strange—not like he usually does. His strides are wider, but slower, and he swings his arms exaggeratedly from side to side. Like a cartoon almost.

He's got to have something left. A guy like that—a guy that's been selling consistently for years—doesn't just up and get "laid-off." Whoever heard of drug dealers laying people off anyway? If you're dealing and you get "laid off," it's usually with a bullet through your brain. I've seen enough movies to know that. He just doesn't want to sell to me. Maybe it's Chuck. Maybe he's punishing Chuck through me. That's not fair at all.

I watch as he makes a sharp right, going down a narrow one-way street. As I make the turn, I realize it's an alley. Doors stand in lines on either side—backdoors—doubtlessly leading into back offices and kitchens of Chinese restaurants, cafes, and apartments. He walks down the line of doors, looking neither to his right or to his left. Just straight ahead—straight ahead at the large steel receiving door that sits on top of a ramp at the end of the alley—at the alley's dead end.

I duck behind a dumpster as he ascends the ramp and knocks on the door's steel. It resonates with a metal clang. It clangs three times with each of his knocks. Then he waits.

Seconds pass, and the door slides open. A bald man in a pin-striped suit slaps Papi on the shoulder and ushers him casually inside. He nods and the man closes the door behind him. I'm overtaken—gone. Curiosity has me in its hold—tight and squeezing tighter—so I make my way closer, using the piles of stinking garbage that litter the alleyway as cover. I doubt they would be of much use if they looked this way, though. From the top of the ramp, you could probably see over everything. But I think I'm fine. I can keep on my toes. The dumpster is safe enough. If the door opens, I'll duck back behind the dumpster again.

I'm close enough now to hear them. They're talking in whispers, and the steel of the door gives their words a strange quality. There's a third one—a younger one. He seems to have some issue with a price.

"That much?" he says.

"That much," the man I don't know answers.

"Colombia. That's where they get almost all of it, and there's a lot of shit going down there these days."

"It's a seller's market."

"Isn't it always a seller's market?"

"Yes, that's correct."

"Fine," the third man says, and then footsteps are coming—quickly.

I stand up and run to the back of the dumpster as I hear the steel sliding door open. When I get there, I don't look—not yet. I don't know if they saw me. I know I'll know soon. I'll know when I hear the sound of a gun being cocked back. Or maybe it's already cocked. Maybe there's already a round in the chamber and they're walking towards me right now. Walking softly—not loud enough for me to hear because I don't hear them. I wait—just a little—as long as I dare, and then cautiously, carefully peek around the corner towards the steel door.

I see the man—the younger third man. He's tall with shoulder-length brown hair and a tan jacket. I can see his purchase, too. It's massive—a huge brick of white and plastic that's crammed clumsily into the interior pocket of his jacket. I'm itching. He's standing on top of the ramp, looking down—scanning. As he walks, he buttons up his jacket. The bulge is prominent, but not too much. Probably not enough for someone to stop him—not enough for someone to notice if they weren't looking.

I crawl behind the back side of the dumpster now. I can hear his footsteps clack clack clacking closer. He walks by me—doesn't stop. He doesn't see. He doesn't see me as he passes by the dumpster and turns right onto the street, his hands thrust casually into his pockets. I peer back towards the sliding steel door. It's closed. I didn't hear it close. I didn't hear its screeching—the piercing sound of metal on metal. I had heard it before, but I didn't this time. Strange.

It's just me in the alley now. I'm alone.

I leave the dumpster and take a right down the street, just like the young third man. I follow him. I have to. I can't let a guy—one guy—get away with that much. The fucker has to be loaded. If he goes down another alley, I'm jumping him—gun or no. I'll take the coke and I'll take his wallet. I can feel the itch crawling up from my toes. There's no cloud in sight. If I can't jump him, I can at least figure out where he lives. I can learn where this much fucking coke is going to be spending the night. I'm sure that's information that Chuck and his buds would like to know. I'm sure they could do something with it.

He stops at a coffee shop that's decked out all in chrome and leather with little tea candles in the middle of the tables. I wait outside and have a cigarette. I watch through the windows as the barista brings him a cup and puts a little metal strainer thing right over the top, filling it with coffee grounds. Then she pours hot water right over. No pot needed, I guess. I bet it'll cost him $9.00. $9.00 for a fucking cup of coffee. I bet he goes into the bathroom after and does a thick long line, too. Fuck, I'm itching.

He takes his own sweet time—sipping slowly like he's in a damn commercial or something—while I go through my smokes. Chuck's probably back by now—hollering and screaming and punching walls. It'll all be worth it if I can get at that jacket pocket. The guy sure doesn't seem anxious to get it home. Taking his own sweet time.

Finally, he gets up from the table. He doesn't head for the bathroom. He goes straight out the front door—straight past me. I stomp my last cigarette into the ground and I'm on him again. Not too close. Just far enough. I can see him, but I'm just another face in the crowd as he turns around and looks. There's nothing to see.

It dawns on me. I hope to God he doesn't call a taxi. If he calls a taxi, I'm fucked. I don't have enough money for fare—not on me anyway. No time to go to an ATM and withdraw the around $80 I think I have. Fuck, I hope he doesn't call a taxi.

He stops and waits for the crossing light. When it comes, he crosses the road and takes a left. I have to sprint in order to catch the light, and I hope he doesn't see me. He doesn't turn around, so unless he has eyes in the back of his head, I think I'm good. He continues walking straight and goes past a small convenience store. He nods like he knows the guy, but doesn't stop.

Now I'm getting tired. I've been tired, but now it's hitting me and I feel like I'm coming up against the wall. *The Wall that Tired Built.* Not a bad title. Tired didn't build it, though. That party last night did. I still feel it in my arms and legs, achiness washing over me in waves tuned to the thump thump of my pounding head and heart. Too much weed and too much vodka. I feel the effort of moving, like if souls had to pull on thick chords and ropes to operate our fleshy sacs—to make them go to the coffee shop and get a cup with a little metal strainer thing right over the top. I'm Sisyphus and my feet are the goddamned boulder.

I hope it's not much longer.

We're in a nicer area now. Not Upper West nice, but nicer than I'm used to. Nice to the 99%. He turns left into an apartment building and I run to catch up. The sign reads Tatar Heights.

The lobby is locked. You need a key card to get in. That's how nice it is. He must have swiped it real quick—had it on a ring or something. The elevator is right along the back wall, and I can see where he's headed through the glass in the door. I didn't really need to see. I could have just guessed. The penthouse. Of course the guy who buys a brick of coke straight lives in a penthouse. Where else?

— — — — — — — —

"Jim's trying to talk to you."

The words hang in the air above my bed like tiny mosquitos, occasionally flitting down onto my forehead or ear and biting—not hard—but enough to keep me awake...enough to leave a mark.

Chuck's asleep. He's been asleep for hours because he falls asleep with that shit flying through him. I'm very much awake. I've been awake.

Jim.

We were at some stupid gas station diner the last time. He held my hand and I let him. I wanted to let him that time because I didn't for most of the times before except for a few. By the lake, for one—just the two of us because his friends had all gone to shoot Luke's .22. My backpack full of stories on lined notebook paper. We held hands and he kissed my neck and I let him kiss there and on my cheek but not on my lips because I was dating Matt at the time. We sat there, underneath an oak tree whose branches hung out over the water and dropped leaves down every few minutes or so because fall was coming. We sat there and he kissed my neck.

Chuck might be dead. I think that every time he shoots up and falls asleep but I think it might be for real this time. I've been watching his chest. It hasn't moved in what has to be a full minute. I keep watching. If it doesn't move for another minute I'll lean over and whisper, "Babe, you alright?" into his ear. A minute after that, and I'll tap him on his arm. A minute after that, and I'll shake him back and forth back and forth until he either wakes up or falls off the bed. After that, I'm gone. I'm picking up my clothes and I'm walking out into the night. I'll sleep on a park bench and come back to the building in the morning. If there are cops out front, I'll never come back again. If there aren't, I'll walk up the stairs to the apartment and he'll be pounding the wall asking where I was. Right as rain.

He coughs, and his chest rises and falls in turn.

I cried in the diner and Jim didn't wipe them. He just let the tears fall down onto my napkin to mingle with the cheeseburger grease. I don't blame him. I never told him how I actually felt. I didn't feel a thing back then. Numb. Numb like Chuck and Jim, but Jim only the one time.

I should try to go to sleep to stop the itching, even if only for a few hours, but I get out of bed and walk out of the bedroom, past the kitchen, to the front door. I walk through, and follow the stairs up to the roof. The access door is supposed to be locked, but it never is. It's always open, so I walk out into the night.

It's still hot and musty from the day, steam rising up from the street and blending with the wisps of cloud that fly by overhead. The black one's out there—getting closer. I can feel it. He's not like the others, casually tugged and pulled by the wind, carried to parts unknown without a care and without will. He's anchored—hard and tight—to me. The winds carry him. He can't avoid that. They lift him up, toss him from side to side, this way and that, but he always centers himself. He always comes back and hovers, descending slowly to steal my air and replacing it with thick reams of smoke. I won't let him have me entirely—not again. I'll take a breath—maybe two—but no more. I'll hold my air in. I'll hold it in as long as I have to—even if it means...

At least I'll die with my own air in my lungs.

Ms. Petersen keeps a lawn chair up here. She sits and reads in it during the day. Her boyfriend was shot during a robbery he botched up so she just sits and reads now. I sit down and lay my head back against the metal frame. I'm so fucking tired, but I know I won't be able to sleep. There's no use in it. I'm itchy all over. It'll be bad if I go another day. That's half the reason Chuck moved over to shooting up. He went without powder for a few days once—when Papi stopped selling to him—and he smashed up the whole apartment. We had to throw out all the furniture. When he wasn't raging, he was staring at the crown molding and sniffling. Of course he got back on coke, and if he ever quits heroin he'll be shaking and vomiting everywhere, but it doesn't look like that vein's drying up anytime soon.

I don't know what I'd be like on withdrawal, but I don't want to find out. I just need a good hit—just one—to keep me going.

Even if I wasn't itchy, I'd be having that nightmare right now. If we had some whiskey I might be able to drown it out. We don't.

I stare up at the blue-black sky and, at some point, my eyes close. I'm not aware of their closing, but they're sealed tight and I drift away to sleep.

I have the nightmare.

We're sitting in a booth at some diner by the water. I told Chuck he needed to get some help, but I haven't told him why yet. He's been begging, but I'm not going to tell him until his friend shows up. I know if I tell him now he'll just try to do it himself so he won't have to share—and probably get himself arrested in the process. It wouldn't be the first time.

I don't know who he's planning on bringing, but I know he has a lot of options. Most of them I've met before—drinking, smoking, or passed out with Chuck with a needle sticking out of their arm. They all have names like Larry or Carl or Pete or whatever. Regular sounding names. They're all fine at a distance, but get too close and they'll start talking about the time their mom beat them with a frying pan or they shoved a broom handle up some girl or smashed a guy's hand with a sledge hammer. They're all troubled one way or another, to put it lightly.

But I don't recognize this guy. Chuck nods

knowingly at him, and he nods back as he makes his way to our booth. Chuck moves over and makes room. They're both sitting opposite me—waiting—but I'm just staring at the guy. There's something about him I don't like. Maybe it's the fact that his hair is shaved down to a burr—like a prisoner's—but I don't think that's what it is. It's not something cosmetic. It's something deeper than that. It's something in the way he absently squeezes his left hand with his right, squeezing in a sort of syncopated rhythm known only to him, or it might be in the way he looks from side to side, like he's waiting for someone. It's 3:30 in the afternoon. We're the only ones in the diner.

"Phil," Chuck says, motioning to the guy, who smiles curtly before his face returns blank. "I know him. He's cool."

"Cool," I say.

"You got something?" Phil says. His voice is high and gravelly. His eyes keep darting around.

"You up for it?" I ask, the implication being, "Are you wasted?" He looks like he could be. His eyes keep darting around.

"I'm up," he says. I don't fucking like him. He looks like the kind of guy who'd kill you for your wallet.

"Lay off it, alright?" Chuck says. "I said he's cool. He's cool."

Whatever. Chuck's doing the work anyway. I guess I have no reason to complain. I just don't want to get a call from him saying that he's at the hospital because Phil stabbed him and took that huge brick of coke.

I take a deep breath. "Alright, so Papi says he's not selling anymore."

"Not even to you?" Chuck says.

"Not even to me. He says he's quitting the business and got some severance package and all kinds of bullshit. I don't buy it, so I follow him. He goes to this warehouse and meets with two guys. There's an old bald one, and a younger yuppie-looking one with brown hair and a beard. Papi and the old guy hand this younger guy a huge fucking brick of powder." Chuck's eyes glow, but Phil's are dead-set on me—staring, vacant, expressionless. I up the ante. "I'm talking about the shit you'd probably see down in South America or something. Massive. Thousands of dollars probably."

Chuck's eyes are wider, but Phil's are exactly the same. That unnerves me a little, but I recover. "So he shoves the thing right into his jacket and heads home—but not before getting a coffee. He goes into a coffee shop with a huge bundle of coke in his jacket! Who does that?"

"Quiet," Phil suddenly says in a whisper, turning in the direction of the kitchen.

Startled, I look over and see one of the cooks, his hair greasy and falling in long strips across his forehead, his face framed inside the tiny slit between the counter and the rack where the order slips are hung. He stares at us, but then picks up a towel and retreats deeper into the kitchen.

"I don't think he heard anything," Phil says, turning back to the table—to me. "Just get to the point."

Chuck's still wide-eyed. I don't think he noticed a thing.

"I know where the guy lives," I say. "The guy with the coke. If we hit him, we'll all get a cut—and I bet there's tons more in his apartment we could grab."

Phil leans back from the table and grunts. "When was this?"

"Yesterday afternoon."

He squeezes his hand, and then lets it linger. "You think he's still got it?"

"It was a lot of shit."

Chuck's been looking excitedly from me to Phil, a huge growing smile on his face. "Damn, this sounds good!" he says.

Footsteps. I look and see the cook—the same one from before—walking out from the kitchen, heading right for us. He's shouting something I can't make out that quickly turns into "Hey! Hey! Where do you think you're going?" as he gets closer.

I look back to the table and see that it's Chuck he's yelling at. He's white as a ghost and frantically climbing over Phil's lap to get out of the booth. I don't know if the cook's yelling or Chuck's running started first, but they're both going full-force now. The cook has the advantage. I can feel my palms go clammy, but I don't move. I just shake—if not on the outside, then the inside. Phil is blank-faced— just his hands squeezing.

Chuck's not fast enough. The cook rounds the

end of the booth and shoves him back down on the seat. "You're not going anywhere," he says, his eyes passing over all of us.

The man starts shouting and I don't know why I look. For some reason my eye just goes there. Maybe it's out of instinct—some childish instinct to crawl under the table and hide. I look below the table and I can see Phil's hands as they unclench themselves and reach into the back of his jeans. His face is still blank—betraying nothing—as he pulls out a gun, all black and metal. His hand tightens around the grip, but he keeps it low—just beneath the table and out of sight—as my heart pounds in my ears.

The cook's words break through. "You have to buy something. I'm not letting you sit here for an hour and a half—taking up the air without buying something!"

Phil casually slips the gun into the back of his pants again. No one notices. No one except me.

"I-I don't have any money," Chuck stammers.

"We'll have three black coffees, the philly cheese steak with fries, the country fried steak, and an order of pancakes," Phil says, turning suddenly to the cook with a smile.

The cook's eyes widen. He nods and walks back to the kitchen, his feet on springs.

Our food comes quickly. The waitress puts it all in front of Phil. He smiles as she walks away. "Now," he says, picking up the plate with the cheese steak and handing it to Chuck, "we're all going to eat our food and calm the fuck down."

He slides me the plate of pancakes. They're dry. There's no syrup on the table but I don't dare draw the waitress' attention and ask for it. I just sit on my side of the booth, my hands at my sides.

Chuck takes a bite of his sandwich and each bite after comes a little easier for him, I think. Phil is cutting huge pieces of his steak, shoving them into his mouth greedily. After a few minutes, he turns to me and says, "Eat," his mouth oozing gravy.

I pick at my plate with the fork.

"We'll hit him tonight," he says, his mouth full and chewing, "—2:30am."

Chuck's elated, beaming. "So you're down, Phil?"

Phil swallows, and nods casually. "Yes, I'm down. Eat your fucking food. Not a crumb, you hear me?"

I dig my fork into the stack of pancakes. The smell and taste is nauseating and I'm not sure why—but I get through. I have no choice.

We go back to the apartment and Chuck shoots up almost immediately. He leans against the wall with his eyes just staring at a newspaper from four months ago, reading the headline over and over:

VEHICLE DRIVES INTO RIVER; FAMILY OF SIX PERISHES

I think I remember the story. It was all over the news back then—not that back then was really all that long ago—but there's a new story out now.

This one's about a shooter who walked into a drug store and shot the pharmacist in the face with a .45. He was her husband and he thought that she was stepping out on him. He drove upstate to a cabin in the woods and, when the police came knocking, he opened the door with the gun in his mouth—blew his brains out right there in front of them.

The car and the drownings aren't as flashy a story. Just a drunk father who was sneaking a flask while his family visited the theme park on the dock—got behind the wheel when he shouldn't. Once it fell into the river, the car got wedged between two dock posts so the doors wouldn't open. It was a freak accident, and it killed all of them.

I just found out today that one of the fancy French restaurants had a strain of Salmonella over the weekend and a bunch of people got sick. I guess that would be today's big story. I doubt it'll last into tomorrow.

Chuck grunts something and Phil bends down and whispers in his ear. Chuck goes white and he's quiet as a mouse after that. Phil isn't shooting up. He's just smoking—smoking like a chimney—one right after the other, letting the used filters fall one by one onto the carpet. I'm not sure why he's still here. Chuck's certainly not much company at the moment.

I'm lying down on a pile of something—clothes probably. It's comfortable enough. I'm just trying not to think—not to think about coke and how amazing it will feel coursing through me. I'm just trying to be, and that's taking a lot of concentration right now.

After about an hour, Phil walks over to me, his face peering down at mine. He's smiling. "What do you saaaaaaay?"

"What?"

"What do you say?" He says with an air of finality.

"I don't know what you mean."

"Did you like your pancakes? I didn't get a thank you."

"Thank you," I scoff. I close my eyes and go back to nothing.

Something—fingers—slide up my leg and graze my thigh. I stand up quickly, but I don't say a word. I'm too shaken—too confused. He stares at me with a strange grin, his eyes almost bugging out of his head. Chuck's already slumped over on the floor—snoring. I won't get help there. I swallow, words beginning to take shape behind my mouth but still all jumbled, mismatched, and unformed. He grabs my side and lifts up my shirt, his other hand still dangling an ashy cigarette.

"Don't," I mumble. It's all I can get out.

"You need to be a little more grateful, I think," he says—hisses almost.

Then it's just like the nightmare, only in the nightmare I'm not in my own apartment. I'm in the backseat of the car with the yellow and the blinking red numbers and the man with the accent and the hat and the pictures of him with the women hanging pinned to his sun visor.

No. I'm wrong. It's not like the nightmare. He stops at the nipple. He pinches it, and drags his hand away. I breathe again.

"Maybe later," Phil says, and flicks the ash of his cigarette down my cleavage before walking out the door, shutting it with a crash.

I fall to the floor. I need my fucking coke.

I don't tell Chuck because of course I don't. Phil's his guy, his special man for the job—handpicked. Even if I did tell him, he wouldn't believe me. Or he wouldn't care—not when that brick is spinning around his head like sugar plums and fucking fairies. I've been out here on my own for almost twelve years now. It's not the first time. Not the first nightmare...

Its 11:00 at night and Chuck's doing the crossword puzzle by the light of his cellphone. It's the only reason we go out and get the paper. He's addicted to the thing. It would be kind of cute if not for the mountains of garbage that make up the backdrop. When he's solved it, he'll just add it to the pile. Someone should clean up, but my arms and legs feel heavy and achy, and I know it's not going to be Chuck. Maybe after tonight. I'll feel better after tonight. Of course, I have to get through tonight first.

"I'm going downstairs, you need anything?" I ask Chuck, mustering the strength to stand.

"What are you going downstairs for?" he asks,

not looking up from his puzzle.

"To get a drink."

"You got money?"

"Yeah."

"Where'd you get money from?"

"Working."

"How much you got?"

"A couple bucks. I'm just going to get a soda."

"Give me $20."

"It's on my card." I walk to the door. I don't want this again. "I'd have to go to the ATM."

"There's one down there."

My hand's on the knob. "No, they moved it."

His eyes close, and then open slowly. He stares at me, his mouth a slit. I can see the anger bubbling up from beneath him. "When'd they move it?"

"I'm not sure. I don't remember."

"I was down there yesterday and it was still there."

"Maybe I missed it then."

"Maybe you did."

I open the door and walk out, his eyes burning a hole in the back of my head. Burning... Another nightmare. The first one.

I go outside and walk to the next building. There's a convenience store on the bottom and I go inside. I'm sure the man at the counter recognizes me, but he doesn't say anything. I don't either. I head to the ATM and withdraw everything in my account except for $2.34. The machine only dispenses $20 bills. I hold the two—not four—bills in my hand and sigh. I'm supposed to get paid this week, but I didn't show up today either and I feel like even if I do tomorrow they'll tell me to go home. I fucking need the money though. Hopefully it's not too late for me.

I grab a six-pack of some brightly-colored energy drink and head to the counter. With one of the bills, I buy the drinks and a pack of cigarettes—whichever brand's cheapest. I don't even check. The man puts them into a bag, but I say I don't need one so he takes them out. I get my change and walk back to the building.

I don't stop at our apartment. I continue on, up onto the roof. I sit down in the lawn chair and smoke and drink the energy drinks. They taste bitter, but I can feel them perking me up a little. I'm going to need them to get me through the night. I just need to wait a little longer—just a little longer and I'll be alright. I just need to get through. I'm not going to look at Phil. I'll just pretend he's not there. When the job's done, I'm done with him. I can remove myself from the situation. Tactically retreat. I doubt there will be another opportunity like tonight. I can avoid him forever—let Chuck have the asshole.

I sit and listen to the sounds of the street for a long time, my eyes not seeing, just looking ahead. In my peripheral I see a tiny shard of yellow. I stand up, look down through one of the windows of the apartment across the street, and see the warm glow of a cigarette. A man is at the end, his head leaning out into the warm air, smoke wafting out. He's in a dark room. His face comes and goes in orange and yellows.

I watch him throw his cigarette down onto the street below and close the window, returning to the dark.

I go back down the stairs into our apartment. As soon as I open the door, Chuck looks up from his puzzle. This is a different one. I guess he had a lot of catching up to do.

"Well?" he says. "Was it there?"

I slam a $20 bill down on the table.

"It's 1:30, now," Phil says. Phil's here. He came about an hour ago and he's been ashing on the carpet ever since. Chuck doesn't stop him. Chuck doesn't do anything—hardly says a word. I don't either. I know that if I open my mouth I won't be able to keep it closed. I can feel my teeth grinding.

"We've got an hour before..." he trails off. "We all know our positions right?"

"Yeah," Chuck says.

I nod. I'm supposed to be the getaway driver. Apparently Phil already has his car parked across the street from the guy's apartment. Ready to go. My only concern is that he might try to stiff us— take it all for himself. I stare at him as he rattles on and on to Chuck at lightning speeds about what to do if the guy resists, if he wakes up, if there are other people in the house. It's making me nervous, but he's getting genuinely excited—frantic even. There's a wildness that's pulsating behind his eyes and tongue. It's more than a little unnerving, especially because I know what he's capable of—maybe even more than Chuck. But maybe not.

Phil puts a briefcase on the table. I didn't know he came in with one. He opens it, and hands Chuck a silver-colored handgun. I start a little. I wasn't expecting this.

Chuck's reaction is worse than mine. His eyes go wide, and he shakes his head back and forth slowly. He tries to keep his composure. "I don't need it," he says as casually as he can, but his voice wavers as he lays the gun on the table.

"Of course you fucking do," Phil answers, picking it up and shoving it into Chuck's chest.

Chuck looks at it, stares, and then looks back at Phil. "No," he mutters, his voice choked, and I'm taken aback. There are tears—subtle but there—and beginning to run down his cheeks. "Not again, Phil. Don't make me do it again...please."

I've never seen him like this before—never. He's open, wounded. I can practically see the smoke in his lungs, the black cloud siphoning down inside. His tears are black and burning.

Phil scoffs, his mouth hanging open. "What the fuck am I looking at, Chuckie?" he laughs, but it's all gnashed teeth and escaping air. He snatches the gun out of Chuck's limp hands. "It looks like I'm looking at a wittle baby."

"I'm not a baby," Chuck cries.

"You sure look like a fucking baby." Phil's drawing closer—inching—forcing Chuck back.

My voice comes, but it's soft and fragile.

"Leave him alo—"

Phil cuts me off. "HEY!" he shouts, turning to me. "You don't want what we're eating. It's not fucking pancakes, I'll tell you that." He grins like he did when he was going up my shirt.

"You said I wasn't going to do it again," Chuck whimpers. "You said—"

"I know what I said, and I meant it—I mean it now." He gives Chuck a hard push, almost toppling him onto the floor. "In case you haven't noticed, we're not going to the grocery store for milk. We're robbing a guy—for coke and whatever else he's got. Now, we don't know what kind of security he's got either and, frankly, we don't have time to find out. It's already been a day, and people don't sit on as much shit as he's got for very long. They unload it pretty quick." He holds the gun out to Chuck, his demeanor soft and kind. "That's why we've got to be prepared, bud."

Chuck's shaking, sweating. Slowly, he reaches out and takes the gun. "You're not going to make me do it again?"

"No. Not again."

They walk over to the table and talk quietly amongst themselves, Chuck warming back to Phil with each passing minute as Phil shows him how the gun works. I don't know what to think, but I know that I see Chuck now in a different light—a two-sided light that somehow emits both the bright and the dark. I think I've always known that was there, but I don't see it often. I saw it once—maybe twice—but there is only one time I remember. It must have been what attracted me to him in the first place—both of us drunk out of our minds after a party and sharing a taxi. It should have been a one-night stand, but it turned into this—whatever this is.

It should have been a one-night stand.

I smoke another cigarette and drink the last energy drink. I'm feeling better now—better with the guns and the crying and the robbery and everything. It's a good thing too, because Phil looks at his watch and his head shoots up and he says "Let's get going!" with a beaming smile, cocking his gun back and shoving it into the back of his pants. He had it out the whole time, I guess.

He turns to me. "Give me your number in case something happens."

The cloud is coming again. "I don't have a phone," I say.

"You don't have a phone?"

"She doesn't have a phone," Chuck says.

Phil stares and then rolls his eyes. "I guess you're on your own then. Probably for the best."

Chuck shoves the gun Phil gave him in the back of his pants and the three of us leave the apartment. Our footfalls down the stairs echo loudly, mixing with the pounding of my blood.

I don't have a cellphone.

We take the subway, and I watch Chuck as the train jostles back and forth on the tracks. It's weird thinking he has a gun on him. I can tell it's strange to him too because he keeps looking around like he knows he's doing something wrong. I'm sure he does. I do, but it's not like we have any other option. We're just trying to get by like everyone else. It's just harder for us.

We get off and walk up the steps into the night. It's quiet, especially for the city. In the distance a car horn blares, but it's faint and seems to bend and fold with the slight breeze. The only other sound is the occasional car driving by. That, and a dog barking.

"This the place, right?" Phil asks, pointing to the apartment as we get to his car.

I look across the road. Tatar Heights. "Yeah. This is the place."

"You said the penthouse, right?"

"Yeah."

"What if he won't let us in?" Chuck asks.

Phil rolls his eyes. "Of course he won't fucking let us in. It's 2:30 in the goddamned morning." He opens up his briefcase on the hood of the car. "That's why we have this." He pulls out what looks like a credit card, but all black.

"Shit, man," Chuck says. "Do they know you have that?"

"It's on loan for something they've got me doing. I figure I might as well put it to good use while I've got it."

"Can't they track it or something, like a log?"

"It'll be fine," Phil says, closing the briefcase and putting it in the front seat of the car. He turns to me. "Don't be playing any games. Stay in the car, and wait."

I nod.

"Don't miss me too much, either" he smiles. He nods to Chuck and the two of them walk across the street to the building. I see him reach into his pocket and draw out the black card. He holds it to the card reader and it beeps faintly. The door opens. They walk inside and a light comes on. It's just the lobby light. Chuck's sweating already. I can see him through the glass in the front doors. His face is glistening. They stop at the penthouse elevator, and Phil brings the black key card out against the reader. The doors open, and then they close behind them.

With Phil out of sight, my edge begins to soften. It comes with anxiety, a feeling of dread I know I should listen to, but I don't. I get behind the wheel of the car and light up a cigarette as my eyes pass over my surroundings. His car is clean—pristinely clean—save for one bizarre feature. There's a pile of ash on the floor of the passenger's side—a literal mound of cigarette ash. It looks like a gray mountain of sand about a foot high. It's unnerving, but I ash into it all the same.

They're taking forever, but when I look at the clock on the car stereo, I see it's only been two minutes. My nerves are getting to me. Who the fuck is this Phil guy anyway? A buddy of Chuck's? If he is, he's not like any of Chuck's other buddies. In some ways he is, but none of his buddies are this professional. They're criminals, sure, but they're not this. This is something else. This is a guy with connections. You'd think a guy like that would have better things to do than go chasing down coke. But maybe not. Maybe that's the similarity to Chuck's other friends: an overwhelmingly thick-headed desire to please. Maybe.

I'm sure of it now. This is taking longer than it should. It's not just a feeling this time. I've been watching the clock. 20 minutes have gone by. That's a long time to be sneaking around someone's apartment. Maybe they ran into trouble. Maybe the guy woke up and tried to fight them off. Maybe one of them is hurt. I hope it's Phil. But then again, maybe it's just taking longer because there's so much stuff. Maybe we'll be rich after this, but I don't think so.

I think they're really in trouble.

Another ten minutes and there's no sign of them. It's coming up on an hour. Maybe they're both dead and the guy's trying to figure out how to dispose of their bodies. I doubt he could call the cops, not with that much coke floating around the place.

Fuck, this isn't good at all.

I feel hot and sticky so I get out of the car and close the door. I check the door over and over to make sure it didn't lock the keys inside. Then I realize I'm holding them in my hand. I pace back and forth. I've got to calm the fuck down.

But they're still not back yet.

I walk across the street to the building and peer through the glass of the front lobby doors. I don't know what I expect to see. The interior is all darkness. The only light is the tiny orange glow of the elevator up button at the end of the room. I know it's locked, but I try the door anyway. It opens. I look at the keypad. It's stagnant, its indicator light humming a bright green. Phil's black card must have done something to it. Broke it.

I walk inside the lobby, but the motion light doesn't go on. Maybe the card did something to it, too. I walk to the penthouse elevator. Surprisingly, the doors are open—beckoning. I step inside into the dark. Not even the buttons are lit, and I grope along the walls looking for them. Suddenly, I hear a sharp snap—just once—and the fluorescent lights above shoot on. My eyes burn, and it takes me a few seconds to notice the large button with the letter "P" printed on it. I hit it, the doors close, and the elevator begins its ascent.

As the floors pass beneath me, I can't help but feel like I've made a horrible decision. I'm walking into danger—knowingly. Best case scenario I'm walking in on a robbery with all that associated risk. Worst case, and this one spins wildly around and around my mind, I'm walking in on a killer. Maybe a drug dealer—just desperate enough to shoot any witnesses. This was definitely a bad—

Ding, the elevator sounds, and the doors open directly into the penthouse interior.

It's a huge open floorplan and Chuck is standing in the center of the room, the gun in his hand and his face flushed and white. The place is all dark, illuminated only by the city light that streams in through the exterior wall made up entirely of curtained floor-to-ceiling windows.

There's a smell in the air I can't place. Chuck looks at me in a panic.

Phil storms out from one of the bedrooms. "What the fuck is she doing here?" he shouts. He doesn't break his stride—walks right up and smacks me hard in the side of the head with his gun.

"Jesus, man," Chuck says, whimpering, "calm down."

I fall down on the marble floor with my back against the wall. I'm bleeding. I can feel the red rushing down warm and slick. Phil's shouting, but his words go in and out. "Gone to shit...fucking had to...all kinds of fucked...where even is it...cops..."

A door begins to open to the right of the room, and both Chuck and Phil turn quiet and stare. It opens slowly, creaking slightly on its hinges.

"Derrick?" a woman's voice calls out, and she steps into the room.

She's wearing nothing but a sheer negligee, her blonde hair falling down in waves across her naked shoulders, shoulders that are smooth and warm. Her lips are parted, and her eyes are bright and gleaming. She's beautiful—perfect.

A warm glow pulses behind her—from a candle on a nightstand next to the bed. I see through the door behind her. A bed made with red satin sheets. A huge painting on the wall. It's nighttime in the image, and a man with a beard and wearing a robe points at a huge column of fire out in the distance.

Her eyes slump downward, and stop at a spot on the floor as she screams.

"No, no, no," I hear Phil say through gritted teeth. His feet are stomping on the hard wood, getting nearer. I stare at the woman as her head explodes, sending shrapnel of skull about the beautiful room, staining her pure white negligee crimson. I'm gone. Out. I'm not here.

Chuck screams at the top of his lungs, his face as red as hers, the noise loud and breaking. He throws the gun against the wood floor. He's shaking with rage, panic, and fear, and points a wavering finger at Phil. "You said this wouldn't happen, Phil. You said—"

"Shut up," Phil says. He's not even looking at him. "Let's see if we can find it, or at least get something worthwhile." He turns to me, and points the gun at a row of cabinets in the kitchen and smiles. "While you're here, why don't you see what's in those."

He goes into the bedroom, and I hear him opening drawers—tearing the room apart. I'm numb again. If the cloud isn't in the room now, feeding us all—me, Chuck, and Phil—that noxious smoke, I don't know what this is. This is death. Her beautiful eyes are still there, and they're still looking at the spot on the floor. I look too and I see the man with the brown beard and the tan jacket, only now his jacket is navy blue. The back of his head is open—red and bleeding. I don't know how I didn't see before.

Chuck is standing in front of me. He whispers, "You better do what he says," and points to the cabinets. The cabinets. I walk over to the cabinets, leaving my mind and consciousness behind.

I open them mechanically. They're mostly cans of food and cleaning supplies, but one has a bunch of medicine. It's mostly over the counter stuff—Ibuprofen, cetirizine—but I take it anyway. As I'm about to close the cabinet door, another bottle catches my eye. Inside are tiny white pills. It's prescription, but I can't make out to whom. The name looks like it's been ripped or maybe faded. I can make out its contents, though. It reads like a thousand knives in my brain. Alprazolam. There's smoke seeping out from the bottle's seal—thick and black. I leave it there.

"Shit-luck," Phil says, coming out of the bedroom.

"You couldn't—" Chuck starts.

Phil shushes him, throwing his finger up to his lips as fast as lightning. The room's as silent as a tomb.

Chuck starts up again. "You couldn't—"

Phil holds out his hand, and we hear them. We all do. Sirens. Soft at first, but growing louder.

"Fuck," Phil says. "We're going."

Chuck nods nervously and follows Phil as he runs to the elevator. I follow too. As the doors close, the woman is staring at me as the red pool at her head grows.

The elevator opens on the lobby floor and the sirens are close. "Who called them?" Chuck asks as we run. No one answers him.

Phil stops at the elevator keypad and waves his black card in front of it. The green light turns red. Once we're outside, he does the same thing on the exterior keypad as Chuck and I run to the car. When we get there, we see them.

Three cop cars round the corner and speed in our direction. Phil gnashes his teeth and makes a break for it, sprinting across the street as Chuck and I climb inside the car.

He opens the passenger door and shouts, "Fucking move!" as his body slams down hard on the seat.

I put the pedal to the floor and the tires screech and the car veers out onto the road and speeds past the three cops. They turn hard, their back wheels sliding. There are only two of them—they must have left one behind—but the two are gaining fast. My eyes pass from the rearview mirror to the road in quick succession as it gets harder and harder to breathe.

"Watch the road!" Phil shouts.

I'm listing to one side, in danger of scraping against the curb. I correct, and make a sharp left turn. I'm not sure where I'm going. I just need them off me. The sirens blaring. That's my only goal. As soon as those two are out of my mirror it'll—

We're in the air, and the car is flipping onto its side, and then onto its roof as we collide against the asphalt and begin to slide. All I hear is the demonic scraping of metal and the blaring sirens. We come to a stop against a light pole—or something. I can't tell. I'm upside down and scrambling frantically to climb out of the smashed up window. When I manage to pull myself out, I see Phil fighting with Chuck. He's not moving.

"C'mon, c'mon, c'mon," he's saying as the cops are getting out of their cars and coming at us with their guns drawn.

"Hands—" one of them says but it's drowned out by the sound of gun fire. Phil's running and the other officer is shooting. For a split second, the one on me turns to look and I run. I run like I've never run before, my heart pounding an anvil of fear in my aching head. The woman's eyes still staring. I hear gunshots—more of them—and I know they're shooting at me now. I try not to think. I just move. I just move as fast as I can.

Footsteps behind me and I push harder, flying down an alleyway. I need an out. There has to be an out somewhere. My eyes scan the doors and windows, looking for one that's open—one that offers escape. I'm getting tired. I don't think I can go on for much longer...

Suddenly, all at once, I realize I don't hear them anymore—the footsteps. I don't know when they left, but they're not here now. I'm alone in the dark alley while some woman yammers loudly on the phone from one of the windows above. Just that and the distant sound of cars in the night.

My hand is shaking and the key is banging around in the hole as I try to open the door to our building. Tears, warm and wet, slide down my cheek and I swipe at them with my other hand as I try to steady the key. I could use the smoking bottle now. That smoke—so thick and black I could almost see the fire underneath.

I get the door open and run up the stairs to the apartment. Once I'm inside, I collapse onto the floor and cry into a pile of old magazines.

Jim had an old magazine. It was his dad's and it had girls on it. The girls leaned over cars and a few of them were washing them with their shirts all wet and translucent and their shirts off when you turned the page. Some of them were washing with their tits. Jim stole it from his dad's desk and showed me. He said they were pretty.

They were all edges and curves and paint. They looked like the cars.

He hands me the paper and I look. It's the face of M. L. Lekesy—my face. I'm smiling in front of a backdrop of blackness while my book floats to the right of me. It's huge with bold, dark letters on the cover that read, "Hard Times in a Small Town." Below that, arrayed in gold, is the coveted accolade, "#1 Best Seller." I can hardly believe what I'm seeing.

"What do you think?" he says, an enormous smile on his face.

It's infectious and I smile, too. "It's amazing," I respond.

"I wasn't expecting to get a mock up, but I guess they sent it as a sort of courtesy. It's great, right?"

"It's amazing."

He takes the paper from me and holds it delicately between his fingers. It's as much of an accomplishment for him as it is for me. The agency has never represented a #1 Best Seller before. I watch as he opens the top drawer of his desk and carefully slides the paper inside. He closes the drawer just as carefully.

"They're saying it'll be up on 23rd and Garden by the end of the month," he says, clasping his hands and resting them on his desk. His smile still hasn't left. "A huge billboard, almost as big as the Linenzombie & Bitch one on 22nd and Azalea."

I feel my heart skip a beat. "That's enormous!" I say, maybe a bit too loud, but I can't contain my excitement. "That's like, what, eight stories tall?"

"Eight and a half," he smirks. "You're big stuff,

Lekesy. Number one for a solid month is nothing to sneeze at." He opens the bottom drawer of his desk and retrieves his day planner. "Of course, we need to keep the fire rolling."

"Of course," I answer.

He licks his thumb and rifles through the pages. I can hear the paper as it flies through his grasp, one page right after the other, and I notice bold numbers flying by. They're dates, filled to the brim with public signings, readings, and media interviews. My heart beats faster.

Being a columnist for the City Tribune, I've had more than my share of public appreciation. The Lekesy Review has won awards for its literary prowess, and Herman Jesinek himself called my insights on the lit scene, "truly revolutionary." But that was me writing about other people's books— other people's genius. *Hard Times in a Small Town* is totally my own, and the result of months of work. Derrick must have thought I was crazy all that time, slaving over the keyboard day in and day out.

"Alright, so Wednesday we've got a reading downtown. Thursday, we're uptown. Friday is midtown with the City Writer's Banquet Meeting in the evening. Then..."

Mr. Greggs goes on and on, and I nod, mentally making note of each and every appearance I'm expected to make. I go through my wardrobe in my mind, walking into the closet and flipping on the light, examining every article of clothing I own and constructing the perfect outfit that fits each event. I remember that it was Karen Sydney who wrote that the wrong outfit sends subliminal signals to a viewer's brain, telling them that the wearer is an outsider, not belonging to the same social class, and thus not worthy of the same attention and esteem as other, more well-dressed guests.

After leaving Mr. Greggs' office, I make my way down Mint St. and shield my eyes from the gleaming light coming from the skyscrapers. I reach into my purse and pull out my Cokelee sunglasses. I put them on and remember how well they frame my face and I wonder what event in the coming week they'll pair best with. I need to remember to re-read Sydney.

As I walk, I think about what kind of impression I'm giving to the people on the street and I expect my meeting with Bryce Holstein to go off without a hitch. The Tribune wants me to interview him on his new collection of short stories by underrepresented literary voices called, *The Unheard.* I'm meeting him at a coffee shop he chose—The Bean. I haven't heard of it, but I'll act like I have. It wouldn't do to have the city's leading literary voice ignorant of local coffee.

I pass 22nd and Azalea and my gaze instinctively goes upwards to the enormous Linenzombie & Bitch billboard. It's a man in his underwear posing provocatively, lying on a leopard skin rug. It looks like something straight out of the seventies, but I suppose that's the aesthetic it's after. I find it gaudy. An image comes to me of the giant naked man looming over the city as its lord. I laugh as I walk by. He doesn't realize that his throne will soon be in contention. #1 Best Seller.

I find The Bean a hip little place on a corner. It looks like any other trendy cafe, but with rusty farm equipment hanging on the walls. That's the only difference. Bryce sits at a table in the back corner and I watch as the barista brings him a cup and puts a little metal strainer over the top, filling it with coffee grounds. Then she pours hot water right over. No pot needed.

I've never seen him before—not even in photos—but I know it's him. He's wearing horn-rimmed glasses, and his hair is cut fashionably, but a bit too long. A little greasy, too, and he passes his hands over his scalp after every second or third sip of his coffee. Black, of course. I've met many writers. They never take cream or sugar.

"Honored to finally meet you, Ms. Lekesy," he says as I arrive at the table, standing up and quickly offering me his hand. "I've read your book and it's really fantastic—amazing, actually."

I nod politely and we both sit down, but he still talks. "The characters, um, especially Dr. Baxter— a"

"Braxton," I correct him, but I don't mind the mistake. He's genuine, and it's actually kind of cute.

"Braxton…" he sighs, and I can see his face turn red a little.

I don't want to embarrass him too much, so I quickly change the subject and pull my pen and notepad out from my purse. "Well, we're not here to talk about me, Mr. Holstein."

"No, no, of course not," he says, recovering

himself a little.

"So, tell me about *The Unheard*."

"What do you want to know?"

I hesitate. "For starters, how about what gave you the idea for the project?"

"Who cares?"

I'm a little taken aback. I don't believe what I'm hearing. "Excuse me?"

He leans against the table, his hands clasped tightly. "Look, I was under the impression that we were going to talk about *The Unheard*."

"We are."

"No, we're talking about bullshit," he says. "It's all fucking bullshit."

I take a deep breathe. "Is now not a good time, Mr. Holstein? We can reschedule." I click my pen closed and start to put it back in my purse when his hand latches onto my arm. It's incredibly hot. I turn to him and remember it. The arm pulling me out of the bed and out of the heat. My heart begins to quicken and I break out in an intense sweat.

"Who are you anyway?" he says.

I've had enough. His behavior is just a side-show now—a slight concern. I remember. It's coming back to me, strong and vivid and horrifying. I can feel my limbs shaking and I can't make them stop. He seems to notice, too, and let's go of my arm in confusion. He brings his hand up to his forehead and rubs it rapidly over and over.

"Jeez, I'm sorry I haven't slept much at—"

I shoot up from the table, knocking over his coffee and spilling it all down my pants. It burns, but I don't feel it. I'm burning inside already, burning with an intense and indescribable fear that's creeping along my spine and shooting down my nerves. I make my way to the door and he trails behind me.

"Where are you going? I'm sorry. Are you alright?"

I hear him calling, but I'm already at the door—pushing on the bar and swinging it out into the busy, bustling sidewalk. I step outside, put on my Cokelee's, and begin to walk, finding the motion easier with each step. Slowly, my breath returns to normal, and a rush of relief washes over me.

In the distance I see the naked king on his rug, peeking out from behind a skyscraper.

I walk into our apartment and evidently the shoot's over. The lights and camera still sit against the far wall, Derrick's designated studio space, and the dead animal carcasses he uses as props are littered about the place. He and his crew and models are all congregating at our center island. All the liquor sits on the counter, most of it empty or in the process of emptying.

A peal of laughter, all that's left from some joke, echoes through the place as my heels clack along the marble floor.

"Oh, thank god you're hear, baby," Derrick says, walking over and kissing me on the cheek. He puts his arm around me, his drink tinkling in his hand, and leads me over to the island where he's placed the printouts from the day's shoot.

"I need your aesthetic eye," he says before turning to his crew. "This is the woman who decides what's art and what's fart!"

They laugh, and I examine the pictures.

He's done something a little different this time. The models are naked and holding the taxidermies up to their lips, making big, comical smoochy lips. There are a few women, but, surprisingly, most of the models this time are men, and most of them are posing with the stuffed beaver.

"Whatcha think?" he asks me, gulping down his drink.

"They're great," I say, nodding as I flip through them, and they are. They might be his best work. "The shadows came out really well."

"I'm sure the Tribune would die to get their grubby little fingers on these, but they're not getting them—not after the stack of pennies they gave me for that batch last November."

"You don't have to bring it up after every shoot, babe," I say, going to the freezer for some ice.

"Hey," one of the models shouts. He's a handsome twenty-something who only bothered to put his jeans back on, leaving his top-half barren. "You know what someone should do? I know what someone should do."

No one's listening to him, but he goes on. He has to be pretty drunk. "People are always counterfeiting hundreds and twenties, right? Yeah, and they're always getting caught because that's what the feds are looking for. Someone should counterfeit pennies, man. Think about it."

He goes back to his drink and seems to get lost in it a little. He stares, watching the bubbles filter upwards from the bottom of the glass.

"What'd Greggs say?" Derrick asks me.

"Nothing," I answer, putting the ice in a glass and filling it with two fingers worth of vodka. "He showed me a mock-up of a billboard for the book."

"Awesome. Look good?"

I nod and sip my drink.

Derrick walks around the island and grabs the photos, looking at them thoroughly. "You know," he says, "maybe you could get these into the Tribune. Work your angle and get me a better deal."

He laughs and kisses my forehead and I smile.

They go on drinking and laughing until late into the night, and I spend most of that time in the bedroom reading a little. I should be reading Sydney in preparation for the upcoming week, but I don't feel up to it, and so I read a mystery novel by Norbert Rob. It's not particularly good, and certainly not enlightening, but it's entertaining and it's the #2 Best Seller.

The panic of the afternoon is far away.

At around midnight, Derrick stumbles into the bedroom. "You still up?" he slurs.

"Yeah, not tired yet," I say, raising my head from the pillow. I had dozed off.

He comes up on the bed behind me and wraps his arms around my neck. His hands slowly, deliberately, sink down onto my breasts. "I guess I've just got to tucker you out, then," he says.

We make love and he's a little drunk so it's rougher than usual. I ball the red satin sheets of our bed up in my fists as the headboard threatens to hit the wall. It never does. When he's through, he grunts and walks to the bathroom, panting softly. I lay my head down on the pillow and put my hand to my chest, feeling my racing heart. It's pounding hard and fast and I can hear every beat in my ears. It's loud, and I wonder if it will slow down or just go on forever. Just as I start to grow worried, I notice the beats dissipate, and the sound fade away. Derrick is pissing into the toilet in the bathroom.

I turn over onto my side and face the wall, exhausted. The sheets are stifling and I toss them away, feeling a cool sensation as the new air touches beads of sweat that have formed on my legs and chest. I don't want to get the bed all sweaty, so I stand up.

My heart fires rapidly again and I hear a piercing scream. I don't know if it's coming from me or from the terrible, familiar thing on the floor by the nightstand, but the terror I feel consumes my entire body and I start shaking violently.

It looks back at me in its burning bassinet, staring at me with flaming eyes, its mouth open and screaming. It's wailing, in terrible pain as its flesh peels off its body and is burnt away.

I collapse to the floor, hysterical and crying, expecting the flames to leap off the burning bassinet and take me next. I long for it. It would mean an end to the dread that's consumed me. It's what I deserve somehow. They don't, but they reach higher, turning the bassinet and the child inside into a smoldering column of fire.

The child's wails grow louder, drowning out even the sound of the flames and the next thing I realize is that I'm in my bed with Derrick over me. A glass of water is against my lips.

"Is this real?" I ask, though I'm not sure why.

"You're fine, M., you're fine," he says.

I drink the water down, and my breathing starts to calm a little.

"What'd you call me?" I ask.

"The doctor said this could be one of the side-effects, remember?"

I don't remember. "No, what are you—"

He walks from the bedroom and I hear him opening one of the kitchen cabinets. I hate that he left me, and I stare at the corner of the wall by the nightstand, expecting the horrible burning infant to return. It doesn't, and Derrick comes back into the bedroom holding a bottle of pills.

He holds it out to me. I see my name on the label.

I'm not on any medication, at least, not that I remember. I think about asking him—asking him what the medicine is for, telling him that I'm healthy and that there must be some mistake. But I'm held back. Maybe there is something wrong. Maybe my memory is failing me. I see it in my mind: Derrick's shocked, confused face when I tell him. It's so real, only a few seconds away. "We can get you some help," he'd say, and then he'd make a phone call. It would be as simple as that. I can see it on his face—the honest fear. It'd be the only outcome. I don't understand.

I just smile.

He puts the pills on the nightstand and climbs into bed beside me. "We can talk to Dr. Braxton about lowering your dosage," he says. "We'll figure it out, babe."

"Okay," I answer, and he starts to snore.

I don't sleep, but stare at the bottle in the dark.

Derrick is out doing a shoot in Granfield Park, and I'm alone in the apartment. I've been sitting on the edge of the bed, my eyes passing from the bottle on the nightstand to the large painting that sits above the headboard. It's of a man pointing to a distant fire that illuminates the night sky. His eyes look directly into the viewer's. It's Derrick's. He brought it back with him from Milan. I think the man is supposed to be Moses.

I check the digital clock on the nightstand. I have a book signing downtown in an hour and a half. I can't stand it any longer.

I snatch the bottle and read the label. At first my eyes pass over the words rapidly, not taking in the information, and then I read again. There's nothing indicating what the medication is, at least not that I can tell. The label is strangely blank, save for the name of the prescriber and an address:

DR. BRAXTON PARKER
1234 TALL GRASS PLACE

The only Dr. Braxton Parker I know is the one I invented—the one in *Hard Times in a Small Town*. Did I get the name from this Dr. Braxton Parker? I don't remember. I don't have the slightest idea because I don't remember ever going to a clinic or getting prescribed anything at all.

I open the bottle and look inside. Tiny white pills—circular and off-putting in a way I can't articulate. I feel a headache coming on and my lungs don't work—like I'm not getting any oxygen. I put the bottle back on the nightstand and drink from the glass of water that's sitting next to the lamp. Only I didn't leave a glass of water out last night. I look and see one of the tiny white pills, its color stark against the dark wood. Derrick must have left it out for me. I get up from the bed and take a shower.

The pill is still waiting when I get out, but I have clarity now. I'm not taking it—not until I know what the hell it is and who gave it to me. I put it back into the bottle and check the clock. I have forty-five minutes to get downtown to the signing. I grab my phone, expecting to see twenty missed calls from Mr. Greggs reminding me to bring some books and the handouts, but there's nothing. Just the time.

I take the subway downtown and the whole time I'm thinking about the tiny white pills. I have the bottle in my bag. Maybe I can stop by his office on Tall Grass Place. Tall Grass... I want him to tell me what they are. I need him to tell me. The subway car takes a few sharp turns as it clacks along the track, and I hear the caplets rustle and jingle from the inside of my purse. I can't shake the feeling that they're an artifact—evidence of something. But I don't know what.

I'm in a haze by the time I get to Cover for Cover, and I barely hear the manager directing me to a table at the front of the store. A cardboard cutout of me—of M. L. Lekesy—is already standing there. It's bright and smiling and everything—everything I'm not. I smile at it, hoping that some of its cheeriness will rub off on me. It doesn't, but I sit down at the table and get out my felt pen anyway. It was a gift from Derrick on my last birthday. My career was already white-hot at the time, so, when he gave it to me, he said, "Here's your carpal-tunnel tool, babe."

When the people come I write the same thing each time. It's generic and safe. "Best Wishes."

I'm only supposed to go till 3:00, and at 2:56 a woman comes up to me and slams my book down on the table. I reach for it, but she jerks it back.

"Excuse me?" she shouts, her face grimaced.

"Sorry," I answer. "Did you want your book signed?"

She just looks at me. Her expression doesn't change.

"I'm the author," I say.

"Who are you?"

I'm getting annoyed, and I reach for the woman's book, trying to point at the author's name at the bottom. "I'm the author," I say again, but she still stands there confused, clutching onto the book like a vice.

"Do you want it signed?" I ask.

Slowly, she nods and hands the book to me. I take it, my pen at the ready, but my grip suddenly fails and the book falls onto the table with a thud. I stare at the cover. It's not my book, but it clearly was before. It was. But this book, the one in front of me, has a deep black cover—dark as pitch—and there's no writing on the front.

"You're the author?" the woman asks.

I open it and flip through the pages, frantic energy bubbling beneath my skin. They're entirely blank—crisp, white. "Where'd you get this?" I ask.

"On the display," she says, and points to the cardboard cutout of me where the bookstore has stacked *Hard Times in a Small Town*. I get up from my seat and walk there.

The manager appears from somewhere off the sales floor. "Three o'clock. Closing time for you," she laughs.

I rummage through the pile of books—my books—except they're all black-covered ones with nothing inside and not my books at all.

The manager starts to help me pack up, taking the black books and putting them in the suitcase I had brought with me. I guess she thinks the store has too many. "Those aren't mine!" I say, and the words shoot out of me loud and strident.

"What?"

I'm panicked, but I try to keep it in check—to breathe. "Someone has switched the books on me, I think."

The manager stops and stands up. She has a puzzled, condescending look on her face. "No one's switched anything," she says.

"These aren't my books," I say.

"They're the exact same ones you've been signing, ma'am," the manager responds. "Now take your things and leave, please. It's 3:10."

"No, they're not," I say, confident that I can convince her. I grab one of the books and shove it into her hands. "Look. There's nothing inside."

She looks at it carefully, flips through a few of the pages, and declares, "No, there isn't."

I start to calm down a little, glad that at least someone can justify me. I'm not crazy. I don't need whatever's in those tiny white pills…

She takes the book back behind the counter and sets it on a shelf before printing out a sheet of receipt paper, the machine whirring as it spits out each glossy inch. She grabs a pen and begins to write. "I'll need to call Greggs up," she says, calm and collected. "I can take a joke—usually—but I don't like him messing with my inventory. This is too much."

My hope drops. "What are you saying?"

She's angry now. "I'm saying that I don't appreciate practical jokes fucking with my business. When I agree to host an author, I expect them to have written something!" She throws the book at me and it hits me on the elbow. "Authors write books, missy!"

I grab my suitcase and run for the door, my vision clouded with tears. As I make it to the street I look backward through the storefront windows. Stacks of black books sit next to the cardboard cutout of me, warped and distorted by the water in my eyes.

I walk for a while, crying.

— — — — — — — — —

I'm at my sister's on the lower-west side, telling her about the black books. I can't get it all out at once. I have to stop to cry. She listens patiently, nodding her head and stroking my shoulder as it heaves with sobs. When I'm finished, she gives me a reassuring smile and gets up from her chair.

Her child, my nephew, is drooling and smacking the carpet with a tiny, plump hand. I watch him for a while, and I can't help but wonder how he can be so content doing nothing.

Janine comes back into the room with a book in her hand. When she sits down beside me on the couch, I see the familiar font and image of a sleepy mid-western town.

"This is your work," she says.

I rub my fingers over the raised letters and read my name, M. L. Lekesy. I read it over and over. With each repetition, I feel more myself.

Her hand is warm and comforting on my shoulder, and I perk up a little.

With a tiny gurgle, William spits up all over his onesie. Janine gasps, then gets up and takes him into the kitchen to clean him off. I stare at the name on the book. The faucet runs in the kitchen, and William laughs as the warm water runs down his chest. I sit as the image of the black, empty book assails me again. For a brief moment, it's more my own than the one on the couch beside me. But the moment passes.

I wonder if I should tell Janine about the white pills.

I hear her take a deep breath and compose herself as she finishes wiping William off. He coos as she brings him back into the living room and sets him down on the floor. Immediately, he crawls off to the corner of the couch he had occupied before, spittle running down his mouth.

I watch as he crawls, scaling the foot of the couch like a mountain and slamming his fat fists onto the cushion. He inches closer to me, gripping the cushions and commanding his wobbly legs to move beneath him. I smile and he smiles back before his eyes fall to the book on my right. I watch his face. At first he seems happy, but a twinge of something is growing, starting at his temples and double chin and working inward towards the center of his face. I can't describe the emotion—the expression—but it doesn't belong on a child. It's not fear or pain, but something else entirely. William starts to cry and I cry too, though I'm not sure why. He looks at me as the tears stream down his face and I feel like we are the only two in the whole world, floating endlessly on a seamless void and crying.

"Oh, come on, Willy," Janine says, scooping him up and carrying him into one of the back bedrooms. I suppose that she is going to feed him.

Before his face disappears down the hallway, I catch a glimpse. The expression—the strange emotion in his face—is gone. He is just a crying baby, and I've lost my only kindred soul.

I don't stay long at Janine's. As the minutes pass, I grow restless, and her smiles are no longer comforting. Rather, they seem desperate—a futile attempt to understand. I say goodbye and leave. It's around six in the evening.

Something is keeping me from going home. I attribute it to Derrick. I know as soon as I walk through the door he'll ask me how I'm feeling just as sweet as can be, but he'll have a glimmer of fear in his eyes when I'll tell him that I didn't take my medication. That glimmer will root around inside of him, festering. It wouldn't be long after that he'd convince me to go out to eat at some trendy restaurant only to drop me off at a psychiatrist's with the parting words, "It's for the best." No, I'm not going home. At least not tonight—not now.

I pass the subway station and keep walking without any real direction in mind, my feet moving mindlessly.

Headlights gleam up ahead in the twilight and a car turns onto the block, accelerating quickly down the street towards me. It's an old car—beat up and yellow. As it passes, I catch a glimpse of the driver.

We make eye contact, and he glances at me through the open window before his face alights with comprehension, a smile creeping out from underneath his long, thin handlebar moustache. He wears what looks like a leather trilby hat, which juts sharply forward as he slams on the brakes, bringing the car to a stop directly alongside me.

"By Chaucer's pokin' stick," he says, turning towards the backseat. There's someone back there. "Do you know who this is?"

He has a strange cockney-ish accent—almost cartoonish sounding. I peer into the car to see who he's addressing. Two young girls, one brunette and one blonde, sit in the backseat. Their hair is up in beehives and they look like something out of the sixties. Their eyeliner is dark and thick, and their lips are painted bright red. They don't answer.

"Oh, c'mon, chums," he says, turning around and smacking one of the girls, the brunette, hard on the thigh. "You know who this is, don't cha?"

She leans forward and turns towards me and I see that her eyes are the most beautiful shades of green and yellow. They seem to flicker and shine, despite the dark interior of the car.

"Well, go on, tell her!" he says. "She wants to hear it!"

"You're M. L. Lekesy, the number one best-selling author," she says slowly, deliberately. "*Hard Times in a Small Town* is a work of genius, a literary achievement crafted by a unique and intelligent voice that truly speaks to the marvels—and the horrors—of the human condition. I, for one, look forward to Lekesy's next work."

Slowly and smirking, she slinks back into her seat while the man laughs uncontrollably. His small frame rises and falls with each sharp peal, and he shoves his fist into his mouth as his eyes begin to water. "Sorry, love," he says between gasps, the sound muffled by his wrinkled hand. "We don't mean to be rude."

At this point I realize that he must be high on something and I begin to walk away—back down the street in the direction I came. I only go a few feet before I turn back around. The car is still running and the man is still laughing and I feel a terrible sinking sensation in my chest. I try to walk away again, but I stop short. I'm unable to help myself.

"What's so funny?" I demand, strutting back to the car. I want my voice to come out strong and fierce, but it sounds like a little girl's.

The man suddenly stops, and his expression becomes as cold and blank as stone. He looks me dead in the face for what seems like ages, throws on a pair of sunglasses that sit on the dashboard, and says, "What's not, baby?" before speeding violently away.

Sometimes I go to the upper-west side and sink into some dance club and just watch people. As a prolific and successful writer, I like to think that you can learn a lot about the human condition by just watching people—being receptive. Inspiration can hit you at any time. There are dry spells, sure, but it comes eventually. You just have to be receptive. Receptivity is everything.

I'm sitting alone in a booth at a popular Latin place, La Casa de la Danza, watching the hips shimmy and gyrate to high-pitched trumpets and steel stringed guitars from my vantage point in the bar's elevated seating area. It's where my walk took me after leaving Janine's. The women are pretty, the men are handsome and ruddy, and I find pleasure in watching them. I check the time and see that it's 1:43 in the morning. The place will be closing soon. I'll need to go home.

Before that though, I order another margarita and pay close attention to a particularly amorous couple on the dance floor. I've been watching them off and on all night, gauging how long the young man's hands linger at the woman's hips—how long the woman allows them to. I wonder, after I leave and go home to Derrick, if the man will walk her home, delaying at the steps up to her apartment complex. I wonder if he'll try to kiss her—if she'll invite him up and into her bed. I wonder.

By the time I walk through the door of the apartment it's 2:30 and I'm tired. I can hear Derrick snoring from the bedroom, and I take my time, pouring myself a glass of water from the sink to wash the tequila taste out of my mouth. As I bring the glass down from my lips, I notice something on the kitchen counter. It's the bottle of pills.

I don't remember leaving them out, and I don't

remember even moving them from my purse. A sickening feeling comes over me as I see a small piece of paper next to the bottle that reads,

TAKE THEM, M.

How did Derrick get them out of my purse? I haven't been home all day. There must be another bottle. I dig into my purse but, no, there isn't. There is only the one and that one is sitting there on the kitchen counter. Does he know I didn't take them? That's impossible. He wouldn't actually count every individual capsule? There must be hundreds of them. I'm starting to panic, and I struggle to move. I feel as if he's standing right behind me, waiting to catch me. It's not even my medicine, is it? I'm not going to take it until I know what it is.

I remove the cap and take out one of the pills, holding it between my thumb and forefinger before throwing it into the sink. It makes a tinny sliding sound as it revolves around and around the drain. Then it finally falls down. It's one less pill in the bottle—if Derrick is counting.

I don't want to arouse his suspicion. I need to be going along with him, so I take a marker out from the drawer and draw a big happy face on the bottom of his note, a sign that I'm cheerfully acquiescing. Hopefully it will set him at ease and set him off of me.

Almost as soon as I put the marker down Derrick lets out an enormous snore. The sound startles me and I quickly look towards the bedroom.

There's only darkness, but, after a few long seconds, I think I see a flicker of light underneath the door. Its faint, but it seems to grow brighter as Derrick's snoring grows louder, more throaty. I realize that the snores are no longer snores, but coughs. They're loud and desperate and I fall to the ground as smoke billows out from the door. The light from underneath the door is bright, and I hear the cracking of fire. The baby is burning.

I'm sobbing uncontrollably, unable to scream or cry out to save him. His coughing grows worse, but I don't hear him moving. How can he sleep? Seconds pass, and I can hear the fire turn into a raging inferno. The coughing is replaced by his screams, and I'm helpless, writhing and crying.

A hand grabs onto me and lifts me onto my feet. Derrick's face is before me, not burnt at all, but soft and concerned. He's speaking but I don't hear the words. I've slipped into hysterics.

"What happened, M.?"

The words break through and I'm sitting in my bed. I'm wearing my night shirt, and my hair is washed. I'm freshly showered. He leans over from his side of the bed, bleary-eyed. "Did you have a bad dream?" he asks.

"Yes," I say slowly. "Yes, but I'm better now."

He mumbles something, turns around, and falls back asleep. As soon as he's asleep I get out of bed and make my way into the kitchen, disoriented and drawn to the last place I remember being. His snoring is terrible to me, and I fear with each peal that it'll turn into choking. When I make it to the counter I see the pill bottle and the note, but it's not the note I remember. Instead of the smiley face I'd written, there's a simple phrase, written in bold, dark letters,

#1 BEST SELLER

My head hurts. I go to bed fearing that I'll have the dream, but I sleep peacefully.

I'm sitting next to the president of the City Writer's Banquet Meeting as the guest of honor. Derrick's seat is beside mine, but he's up taking pictures of some of the industry bigwigs. What he's working on now is a series of black and white portraits. "Missteps," an attempt to capture what he calls "the unconscious, in-between emotions." In practice, he's pricking famous people with needles and photographing their spontaneous reactions. He's already received a few grants...and a few bruises.

Mr. Greggs is seated at a table near the front with his wife. He gives me reassuring glances.

The recipient of the Rising Star Award for Best Student Writer gets up to give his acceptance speech and I quickly rifle through my own, mentally noting each point that I'll touch on. Being the guest of honor at the annual dinner is nothing to take lightly, and I really want to make a lasting impression. Most of the literary world—at least the ones that matter—attend the dinner, and I know they'll be influencing my career for decades to come.

Despite the pressure, I'm confident—even excited. It's the first time in a long while.

The president gets up and I smile as he walks over to the podium. He gives me a look and I practice the breathing exercises my yoga instructor taught me—eight seconds in, and eight seconds out.

"Our honorable guest of honor tonight is a woman that truly deserves all the honor we can bestow upon her," he says, pausing for dramatic effect. "She's a #1 Best Seller."

He turns and looks into my eyes as he continues. "*Hard Times in a Small Town* is a work of genius, a literary achievement crafted by a unique and intelligent voice that truly speaks to the marvels—and the horrors—of the human condition. I, for one, look forward to Lekesy's next work."

I stand up and walk to the podium as the president gives me a nod. I'm flustered—I recognize the speech—but I try to shake it off as I lay my notes out on the podium and clear my throat.

I look up to the crowd, their faces eager and expectant, and look down at my notes. I feel my vision blur and my pulse skyrocket. The pages are entirely blank. Somehow I must have carefully folded three empty sheets of paper, and carried them around in my coat pocket for the entire evening. But that's impossible. Just minutes ago I was going over them—bullet point by real, actual bullet point. I must have left them over by my seat. I glance over and see Derrick smiling. From the podium, I quickly scan the table and under my chair, but I don't see any loose pages. I don't have time. I don't have time. The faces are starting to grow concerned. I open my mouth and say the only thing that comes to me. I say it solemnly.

"#1 Best Seller."

As I'm waiting to think up what to say next, a man stands up in the back row. I can't make out his features. He begins to clap—slow at first, but his speed quickens. Several others stand up, joining in his clap, and soon roaring applause fills the dining hall. I smile—disoriented—my eyes fixed on the man in the back as my vision adjusts to the bright lights overhead. I notice that he's wearing a leather trilby hat, and has a handlebar moustache. He grins a grin I recognize and my mind goes blank.

The president comes to my side and gently nudges me down from the podium. "M. L. Lekesy, everyone!" he says, and the audience cheers again. Unsettled, I walk back to my seat.

As I sit down, Derrick leans over to me and whispers, "That was fantastic, baby."

He turns back to the podium as the president introduces the next speaker. I don't look. I watch Derrick as his face fades to indifference, as the president drones on, and as his hands come to together to clap while the next speaker walks onto the stage.

After the dinner, and after some of the

formality has died away, people begin to abandon their tables and walk the room freely. Derrick kisses my cheek and walks toward the back, his camera primed and ready. I sit alone and smile as the faces walk by. One comes up to me.

"Brilliant, brilliant," it says.

I stand and smooth out my dress. "Thank you."

He points his finger at me and winks his left eye before giving me his hand. "K. R. Kingsley," he says. "Pleasure to make your acquaintance. I'm a novelist, too."

"Oh, really? What have you written?"

"Nothing as good as your stuff." He smiles, but it's uncomfortable. "We try though, right?"

I try to lift his spirits. "I'm sure it's great."

He laughs. It frightens me, my ears ringing loud and strident. A stream of spit slinks down his chin. "You'd think so, but it's not. How could it be?" He's shouting now. "HOW COULD IT BE BETTER than *Hard Times in a Small Town*?"

He stares at me, his eyes wild.

"Okay," filters out from my lips in a sigh and I'm nodding like a mad-woman. I sit back down and stare at my napkin on the table. A hand is thrust into my face and I shake it.

"Brilliant speech," a man says. He's wearing a suit, and his hair is cut very fashionably. "I'm a writer myself."

"What do you write?" I ask. We're still shaking hands.

"A little of this, a little of that—anything by H. J. Benjamin," he laughs, his eyes wide.

"That's you?" He's friendly, and I'm calming down somewhat.

He points at me and winks his left eye before blending back into the party.

Kingsley is still staring at me—standing stiff as a board and smiling. I feel lightheaded so I leave the table for a drink, trying my best not to look at him. I wait in line at the bar and try not to look at anyone, feeling Kingsley's gaze boring into the back of my skull. When I get to the front of the line, the bartender asks what I want.

"Anything," I answer, and I realize that my voice is the only sound in the room. The bustle of the party has completely died. It's utterly silent. I turn around and now every eye is on me, staring and smiling just like Kingsley as if they're expecting me to speak—as if they're waiting for me to do something. I'll do it. I'll say it. Whatever it takes to make them go away. The only thing that comes to me is "#1 Best Seller." As the words leave, the mustached man in the leather trilby is the only one who moves, pacing and chuckling quietly to himself in the back of the room. The rest are as still and as silent as stone.

The crowd parts and a young man comes forward. Still yards from me, he offers his hand and continues walking. That blank stare and smile.

"Miss?" the bartender says behind me, nudging my elbow.

Startled, I turn around and the martini he's made spills all over my dress.

"I'm a writer. The name's T. J. Tanner," the

smiling young man says, in front of me now, reaching for my hand.

"It's nice to meet you, but I've got to go wash up," I say frantically, grabbing a napkin from the bar and wiping my dress.

"Brilliant, brilliant," I hear him say as I walk out into the hall, and I think I hear the words repeated in a dull chant by the rest of the crowd.

I think I'm slipping.

I go into the women's room and splash water onto my face. The lighting is dark—almost ambient—like in a fancy restaurant. It's coming from two large wall sconces, and the walls behind them are painted a dull shade of crimson.

Over the sound of the open faucet, I hear the toilet in the stall closest to me flush. I grab a paper towel to wipe off my dress and run it under water as the woman in the stall comes over to the sink beside me. I glimpse her in the corner of my eye and back away, her beehive hairstyle bobbing in the mirror as she washes her hands. It's the brunette from the car—unmistakably.

"You're a board member?" I ask her.

She smiles, coyly almost. "And you're a famous author." She laughs a little—a high, tinny laugh—as she dries her hands. I'm staring at her, and she notices. "Don't be wondering who I am, sweetie. It's you who should be concerned."

"I'm not dreaming," I say. "I'm—"

"A #1 Best Seller?" she throws the paper towel into the trash and turns to me. "I've heard it before, Marie."

"I'm M. L. Lekesy," I say, but she's gone. All that's left of her is the slight swinging of the bathroom door.

— — — — — — — —

I'm on my way to a book signing—this time on the lower-east side. It's the first one since the black books, and I hope to God that I don't have some prankster following me around—that this one will go smoothly.

I'm on the subway train. Sometimes I like to go underground, away from all the loudness of the city streets. Everyone's always silent on subway cars. There's just the sound of the train and the clacking of the tracks and the scratchy intercom voice. The intercom voice is the only bad part about the subway, but I find solace in imagining what kind of person that chirping, robotic voice belongs to.

I got a lot of the ideas for *Hard Times in a Small Town* from the subway. I think it gave me reprieve enough from the bustle to think, but was still close enough to people for me to get inspiration. It was a kind of sweet spot. But lately I've gotten nothing from my subway rides—just the engine, the tracks, and the disembodied crackling voice.

I reach into my purse and get out the pills. The bottle's about half-full—not because I've been taking them, but because I've been meticulously tossing a pill a day into the garbage disposal. Derrick doesn't seem to have caught on. I examine the label again. I hate looking at them, and I look with a kind of detachment because I know they're not me. I don't need medication, and I never have. I'm a unique and intelligent voice.

Still, I need to figure out why they're in my name, and why Derrick is so convinced I need to take them. I'm not sure why I don't already know the answer. I can't imagine not being privy to that information. Maybe I forgot—people forget—or it's just a big misunderstanding. Dr. Braxton will know—if the guy exists.

A thought hits me and the pieces fall into place. There is a Dr. Braxton, but he's the one I invented. Someone is playing with me, posing as a doctor and trying to get me to take these pills. Maybe they're roofies, and they're trying to drug me up and have their way with a famous novelist. Some kind of crazy fan. They must have called the apartment and given Derrick a good show. He's all convinced.

I breathe a sigh of relief, the first one in a long time, and listen to the clack of the subway train. My mind goes to the brunette with the beehive hair, and to the man with the leather trilby. It had to be one of them. They're straight up weirdos.

Such is the price of fame.

"Next station is Mulberry. Doors open on the right," the crackly voice declares over the PA system. I wonder what its owner's favorite color is.

I get to the place and, for about the first half-hour of the signing, I'm terrified that someone will come up to the table and hand me a blank, black book. I flinch with each new person, but I eventually calm down as every familiar copy of *Hard Times in a Small Town* slides in front of me.

I leave the bookstore at 4:45 to find Mr. Greggs waiting for me outside.

"Pardon me, Miss," he says, putting on an odd voice as if he was someone else. He laughs at his joke.

I stop in my tracks. "Mr. Greggs, I didn't know you'd be here."

"I couldn't keep myself away," he smiles. "All the art columns in all the papers tell me that this is the place to be."

"There's got to be one that doesn't."

"Not that I could find." He starts to walk away, but stops and turns toward me. "Do you want to get a drink? I have some very good news, and good news goes best with good brews."

"What news?"

He winks his left eye and points his finger at me in a knowing way. "Come on. I'm parked over here," he says, and cocks his head in the direction he's walking.

I follow him, expecting some light conversation, or a hint as to what his news might be, but he remains silent. It's entirely uncharacteristic of him, and puts me on edge.

"Where did you want to go?" I ask, looking for anything to break the silence.

"Doesn't matter," he replies. "Just as long as they've got brews for my news."

We walk a few blocks and turn into a public parking garage beneath a SleepInn hotel. Mr. Greggs' footsteps resonate on the damp concrete, echoing loudly.

"You didn't have the chauffeur wait for you?" I ask.

"Nah. I like to drive sometimes. Here we are," His face lights up and he starts walking towards the elevator in the middle of the garage. He hits the up button and the doors open. He motions me inside and I step in as he follows after me. The doors close, and, for a few brief seconds, we're alone in the dark.

"Fucking light's out again," he says.

In the dim light, I see him raise his hand and put his thumb and middle fingers together. He snaps, and immediately the light on the ceiling comes on. Aghast, I stare as the bright florescent light casts strange shadows on the lines of his face, making him look ancient.

"I'll take care of you, Lekesy," he says. "There's a lot more where that came from."

He puts his hands behind his back and looks ahead as the elevator hums to life. I laugh. It's a bit. "How many times have you done that? You always park in this garage?"

He looks at me and smiles.

We get off on the third level and walk to his car, a bright red sports car with a vanity license plate that reads "SPR8GNT." He opens the door for me and I get inside.

We drive downtown, barely saying a word and still with that strange, uncharacteristic stoicism about him. I feel like, despite what he said, the news must be bad.

I can't stand the suspense. "Everything

alright?" I ask.

"Just fine, Lekesy."

We get out at an upscale place—one I've never heard of: The Blue Clam. A valet parks the car, and Greggs straightens out his jacket.

"Am I dressed alright?" I ask him. I'm wearing a professional looking pantsuit—business appropriate, but not at all formal.

"We'll be fine," he says, and motions me inside.

The restaurant is dark, and looks to be lit by only candles that sit in the middle of the tables. The walls are painted red, and old Victorian-looking paintings hang on them—portraits mostly, interspersed with a few landscapes and statues.

The maître d' comes up to us, smiling and friendly. He looks at Greggs, who nods, and then leads us to the back of the restaurant.

We walk up a single step and arrive at the back wall. "I'll leave you to it," he says.

"Thanks, Jeffrey," Greggs says. He looks around cautiously and walks towards a replica of Michelangelo's David. Quick as a flash he grabs David's penis and testicles in his hand and gives them a sharp clockwise turn, looking me in the eyes as he does it.

The wall to the left of the statue pops inward, and Greggs puts both his hands against it, sliding it open.

"News and brews," he says, touching my shoulder and pushing me into the space where the wall used to be. I resist at first. I've never seen anything like it. It's like some old-timey detective movie.

It's dark, but I can make out faces. Greggs closes the wall behind us and they dissipate into the impenetrable blackness. A click and a light comes on, flooding the small room.

The men—four of them—are all in suits, sitting around a large poker table. Most of them are smoking cigars or drinking whiskey, but they put down their smokes and drinks as Greggs motions for me to take a seat at the table beside them. He sits down next to me. I nod to them nervously— terribly confused. Greggs smiles like a little boy, his moustache high up on his cheeks.

He says, "News…"

And a tall brown-haired man who looks to be in his fifties pulls a six-pack of High-Times out from underneath his chair, slamming it down on the felt top of the table. "…and brews," he replies.

The mood turns immediately casual, and the brown-haired man stands up and offers me his hand. "J. L. Harkins," he says. As I take it, I recognize the name.

"You've got to be kidding me," I say. I try to keep my amazement in check, but it comes out strong in my voice.

"I'm not," Harkins says.

"But you never make public appearances."

"News and Brews is hardly public."

"But you're the author of *The Whole Nine*. I had to read it in all my Lit Theory classes. It's brilliant."

"Thank you."

"No one can ever get a word from you—none

of the papers can."

"Contain yourself a little, Lekesy," Greggs says, his smile beaming. He reaches out and touches my shoulder and I wake up from my J. L. Harkins stupor. "There's some others I'd like you to meet."

Another hand is in front of me, and I shake it. "H. T. Derr," its owner says.

"Shut up," I say. "*To Be an Ostrich?*"

"Yep. That's me," Derr replies.

Greggs tugs at my arm. "And…"

I recognize the next man without needing an introduction. "J. T. Studebaker!" I scream, and immediately feel incredibly embarrassed. "I'm so sorry."

"Don't be. I'm used to it," he says. "I'll probably need a hearing aid by the time I'm thirty-five, but 'tis the price of fame."

"I adore *The Shoe's On the Right Foot*," I say with almost religious fervor.

"Everyone does."

"Modesty is not Mr. Studebaker's strongest virtue," Greggs says.

They laugh and I stare at each one of them, dumbfounded to be meeting three of the greatest literary minds at the same time and in the same room. My gaze passes to a figure that remains silent to the right of Mr. Greggs. He's wearing a matching black suit and tie, and dark sunglasses.

"Oh, don't mind Flameo over here," Studebaker says.

"No," the dragon says, "please do."

Flustered, I stand up and shake his hand. I'm

self-conscious about my grip, but try to match his the best I can. His scales are cold and hard. He doesn't smile or nod, but stares at me as smoke pours out of his mouth.

He gets down on one knee and bows his head towards me. Harkins, Derr, and Studebaker get up and do the same while Greggs stands to the side of the room and smiles. I see a single, solitary tear roll out and slide down his cheek before falling to the floor.

They begin a sort of chant. "You are one of the fold, M. L. Lekesy. You are one of us. You are a #1 Best Seller."

I spend the rest of the evening with them. At first I don't believe it, but, by the time Mr. Greggs bids his goodbyes and we leave around 11:00, I do.

─ ─ ─ ─ ─ ─ ─ ─

I can hear the boom of the music before I even get out of the elevator and I know that Derrick is having one of his infamous parties. The idea of rubbing shoulders with the city's elite always excites me, and I practice my smile before I walk inside, remembering that it was at one of his parties that we first met.

"Hey, do I know you?" he had asked over the music.

"Not yet," I replied.

He picked up on the subtle flirtation in my voice, and we started going steady less than a week later. Things are perfect with us.

I walk through the door and the music bombards me, loud and pounding. I see Derrick's hand rise up over the crowd and he waves me over to him. He smiles and I slide against his shoulder and we dance and grind on each other's bodies without saying a word. I can tell that he's been drinking, but he's by no means drunk. He's never drunk. He handles his liquor well.

We dance and I think I see a leather trilby pop up over the heads in the crowd. It sets me on edge. But, as the disco lights Derrick installed last spring change to bright red, I realize that it's not leather at all, and that it belongs to a portly clean-shaven man.

"What's the matter, baby?" Derrick says, kissing my neck.

"Nothing, I guess," I answer, but I'm still perturbed and my mind goes back to the pills. I lean in close to his ear and whisper. "Have people been calling the apartment?"

"People call all the time. Have you been expecting someone in particular?"

I speak slowly. "Does Dr. Braxton call?"

"Not since he got our address."

"What'd he need our address for?"

The music picks up and Derrick leans in closer. "What?"

"I said, what does he need our address for?"

"He said something about the office not getting it right."

He's moving around me to the music, but I stand in my place. "Did we ever talk about me visiting Dr. Braxton?" I'm trying to break into

Derrick. I want to show him some kind of discrepancy. I know there is one.

He looks concerned. "We all did—the whole family. We were worried about you after what happened."

I feel immediately warm and I start to sweat. There's a door in front of me. Crackling heat dancing along the floor. I bring my hands up to my temples.

"Actually, I don't think we did," Derrick says, smiling, and I'm back in our apartment with the music pounding.

I'm gasping, and the air isn't coming easily, but he doesn't seem to notice. "We never mentioned it, then?" I ask.

"Yeah, I guess not."

"Then why is it so important to you that I take my medicine?"

"I just figured that, if a doctor prescribed it, you probably need it."

"Did you even check to see what it was?"

He looks at me, points, and winks his left eye. "You're a #1 Best Seller, babe. I trust you."

That night we make love and he's as gentle and passionate as usual.

I drive upstate to the miles of farmland that stand between the city and the pacific on the other side of the country. I can't help but take in the scenery and be depressed by it. There are buildings everywhere that have no business standing. They lean awkwardly to one side, sometimes even threatening to touch the ground. Their roofs are black as tar and full of holes. Even the trees are sickly. Though they litter the countryside they're no taller than my knee, with bark that's gray and flaking, surrounded by tall grass that writhes in the wind. Tall grass...

Everything seems to be standing around, wondering why it doesn't just blow away.

The people have it the worst. Their eyes are sunken deep into their skulls, and their mouths are always open. They shamble down their dirt roads and tall grass and wave to everyone they pass with a smile as big and dumb as their oversized t-shirts. They lean over their cars and drink beers and yell at their family members in-between crass jokes. I've never seen one do a single interesting thing, but I make a point not to see too much of them. I'm only passing through.

It seems like eons by the time I arrive at Dr. Liam's property. It's an enormous villa that sits on top of a hill overlooking the blighted countryside, a shining beacon of hope and civility among the lost and the damned. As I pull onto his cobblestone driveway, I can't help but be overwhelmed by the enormity of the place—like I am every time I visit. I feel a little envious. There's simply no space for such a big place in the city, but I'm comforted by the fact that at least I'm surrounded by real, engaging people and not nothingness.

Dr. Liam likes his privacy, and I can't blame

him for that. His studies require intense concentration and the bustle and excitement of city-life would be too much of a distraction. There are no distractions in the countryside. There's nothing.

I park my car in the driveway and walk up to his front door. I ring the bell and wait, reaching into my purse to check that the bottle of pills is still there. It's resting peacefully on a tampon wrapper at the bottom.

The door opens and Dr. Liam's face is beaming back at me. I expect him to be morose, but that must be the countryside getting to me.

"M. L. Lekesy," he says, "it's fantastic to see you!" He leads me inside his house and I examine it for any changes.

Everything looks the same since the last time I was here. The walls are in a modern, minimalist style, decorated only by the dozens of awards and medals Dr. Liam has won throughout his prestigious career.

"I only need the Nobel," he says sullenly as we walk into his living room. He says it every time I visit. He goes into the story, but I can recite it almost word for word.

He was born in the city to a wealthy hotel mogul back before the government had monopoly laws. He grew up as wealthy and as privileged as they come, but was never jaded by his life of luxury. He always dreamed of giving back, and so, when his father died, he spent his portion of the trust fund buying all of the technical and scientific instruments he could get his hands on. He read every book, attended every lecture, and interviewed thousands of the world's great scientific minds—all for the singular goal of curing cancer. He firmly believed that all that was lacking from the efforts of the minds before him was the proper start—the start that an 84 million dollar fortune could afford.

He hasn't cured cancer, but he's found plenty of ways to deal with AIDS. The Tribune did a write up on him last year, and rightly attributed the 38% drop in AIDS-related fatality to him. It's his finest achievement, and it's won him hundreds of awards.

"I only need the Nobel," he says.

He motions for me to sit down on the large, red chaise couch against the wall on the right side of the room, and I do. He takes the green suede recliner opposite.

He's about to speak when the front door opens. We turn our heads in unison as Dr. Liam's wife bolts through the opening, dressed in a pink blazer and matching skirt, her heels clacking against the tiled floor. She's a Swedish blonde. Last year, while incredibly drunk at a party, Dr. Liam admitted that he had only married her because she was the daughter of one of the Nobel electors.

She stands in the foyer and reaches down to take off her heels, her jaw flapping a thousand times a minute as she chews her gum. Her driver darts past—not saying a word—as she peels the sunglasses off her face and looks into the living room.

"I wasn't expecting company," she says.

"It doesn't have to concern you, Bianca," Dr.

Liam replies. "M. Lekesy is just stopping by."

I'm expecting her to run over to me, squealing. She has to know who I am. She just stands there.

"Do you do any reading?" I ask her politely.

"Don't bother," Dr. Liam interjects. "Swedish soaps are about as cultured as she gets."

I look at her as she walks deeper into the house and I wonder how she exists. Maybe it's the writer in me, but I wonder how she can go on living a life of vapidity, devoid of any real beauty or meaning. She makes me sad, and I feel for her.

"What's that you've got there?" he says, looking down at my hands.

I look and notice that I'm clutching onto the bottle of pills. I don't remember getting it out of my purse. "It's the reason I'm here," I tell him. "I want to know what they are."

He reaches out and I hand him the bottle. He lowers his glasses down from the top of his head and examines the label. "Doesn't say what it is."

"No."

"Why don't you ask this Dr. Braxton fella?"

It's an obvious suggestion, but I can't explain why the idea fills me with dread. I've been planning to pay Dr. Braxton on Tall Grass Place a visit for days, but, with each day that passes, I feel more and more incapable. I can't do it. I won't.

"I just need to know first," I say.

He opens the bottle and takes out one of the pills, holding it between his thumb and forefinger. "Why'd he give them to you?"

"I don't remember."

He looks at me and I regret coming. This was a stupid idea. He drops the pill back into the bottle, closes the lid, and hands them back to me. "These aren't yours, are they?"

"What?"

"You're looking out for a friend."

"No, no. They're mine." I turn the bottle in my hand. "My name's on them."

I read every word, my eyes darting frantically. My name's not there. There's only Dr. Braxton Parker and the address.

"I didn't see a name," he says.

"I guess I was wrong." I don't leave the bottle, and I feel like I can see faint shadows of letters breaking through the white of the paper. When I blink my eyes, they disappear.

"Are you alright?" he asks.

I look up at him and smile. "Yeah, I'm fine."

"Who are the pills for?"

I feel exposed, and my eyes dart about the room. My vision is blurry—blurry with smoke. It comes back to me in full force as terrible as ever. I need to calm down, but I can't with Dr. Liam sitting at the edge of his chair, his face haggard and concerned, barking at me, "Whose are they? Whose are they?"

"I need to go," I say, standing up and slinging my purse around my shoulder.

"So soon? I thought you wanted to know what's in the pills?"

"I do, but not now. I'm sorry."

"Well, just give me one," he says, holding out

his hand. I unscrew the lid and drop one of the tiny white capsules into it. He's not as concerned for me after that.

I open the front door and he follows after me. "I'll test it and call you with what I've found," he says. I can tell he's looking for some sign of recognition from me.

I nod as I walk out the door.

━━ ━━ ━━ ━━ ━━

I wake the next morning to Derrick huffing and muttering under his breath. He's moved the photos and lamp from the nightstand and I hear him banging and scrounging around the cabinets in the kitchen.

"Babe?" I call out, my eyes still closed.

"Yeah," he answers. He sounds out of breath.

"What are you doing?"

A huge crash sounds and I rise up in bed with a start. "What's going on?"

I walk out into the kitchen. Derrick is slumped over on the floor, sweat pouring. His face is grimaced, and his eyes are red with tears.

I run to him. "What happened?" I try to stay calm, but I'm terribly scared.

"I can't find my fucking pills," he says. "I need my medication."

"What medication? You never told me you were taking anything."

"I didn't want you to worry. I told Dr. Braxton not to call."

I can't believe what I'm hearing. "Do you mean my pills?"

"What?" he mumbles. I don't know what's wrong, but he looks like someone with a high fever—slipping in and out of consciousness and fading away.

I go to my purse on the counter and pull out the pills.

"That's them," he mutters. "Why'd you have them?"

He raises his arm—pleading—but I don't give them to him right away. I turn them in my hand, reading the label.

PRESCRIBED FOR: DERRICK M. MULLIGAN

"Fuck it, M., just give them to me!" he howls, and I hand them over. I'm trembling.

He undoes the cap and pops two of the small, white tablets into his mouth, swallowing them dry. Almost instantly, it seems, he's better. His breathing regulates, and the glistening sweat that covers his body starts to dry. His eyes lose their redness, and his skin regains some of its color. He looks up at me.

"Why'd you have them?" he asks, his chest heaving.

"I thought they were mine."

"Why the fuck would you think that?"

"You told me they were."

He lifts himself up off the floor and walks

slowly into the bedroom. He's upset with me. I can tell by his face and by the way he slams the bedroom door shut. I hear the shower run, and I sit down on the kitchen floor and cry.

I ride the elevator up to the 23rd floor. Everyone at the agency recognizes me as I walk through the office. They smile and nod and I can see their faces perk up as I pass. It's a good feeling. I walk into Mr. Greggs' office. He's slouched over his desk but stands up as I enter into the room. He says nothing, but smiles and motions for me to sit down at the chair. I do, and he sits down after me, looking mischievous, like he's about to play a practical joke.

"Why did you want to see me?" I ask.

Still smiling, he opens one of the desk drawers, retrieving a large manila envelope. He slides it over to me. It's addressed to the agency, but it has my name on it. I look at him.

"It's open," I say.

"Just read it."

I reach inside and pull out a thin sheet of paper. There's only a few paragraphs typed out in bold Times New Roman. I read them, but my vision blurs with excitement and I'm forced to read them again in order to fully take in the words.

"This can't be real," I say.

"It can," he says, laughing, "and it is."

I read the first sentence aloud. "This letter is to

inform you that, in light of your recent literary achievements, you are being awarded the Nobel Prize in Literature."

"Words have never sounded so sweet, huh?"

"I can't believe it," I laugh. I can feel tears forming in my eyes, and a rush of emotion washes over me. Everything I've worked for—the hard hours at my computer, my years of striving to understand the nuances of the human person—all of it is paying off in the biggest way imaginable. I say the words in my head over and over: Nobel Prize Winner.

"It's like I always tell you, Lekesy," he says. "You've got the stuff."

"The ceremony is next month. You're coming with me, right?"

"Of course. And the News and Brews boys will be there too. They wouldn't miss it."

This was all feeling surreal. My biggest literary idols would be in the audience as I received the world's most prestigious literary award. "I don't know what to say."

"Don't say anything then," Greggs says. He winks knowingly and snaps his fingers.

—————————

The waiter refills my mimosa for the second time and I take a large sip. I'm feeling a little heady, but the brunch so far has been pretty boring and I need something to perk me up. All of the speeches sound the same. I guess it's indicative of the famine of originality in the literary world.

I check my watch. There's only two hours left, but they'll linger for as long as possible. It'll seem like ages. I know I owe the publishing house immensely for getting my work out there, but all of the other authors they've published fail to excite me and I'm tired of listening to them drone on, praising Preston Publishing as if their life depended on it.

Derrick decided not to come with me, and that's alright. Ever since the incident two days ago I look at him differently. I'm not sure how much is him and how much is his medicine. I didn't know he needed medicine, but it makes sense. I guess he was trying to convince me it was mine out of some weird cognitive dissonance. It was awful of him. I don't know what's in those pills, but I'm sure they're dangerous to take if you don't need them.

My phone vibrates in my purse and I get up from my seat and walk out into the foyer of the restaurant, more than happy to get a few minutes' repose. I take my drink with me.

Once I'm in the hall I answer the phone, speaking a little quieter than usual so as not to disturb the plump middle-aged man who's taken the podium—just so pleased that his science fiction novel was published through Preston.

I don't recognize the number, but I know the voice as Dr. Liam's. "M?" he says. "I've got the results you wanted."

"What results?"

"Derrick's pills."

I never told him the pills were for Derrick. I

didn't even know at the time.

"Are you still there?" he asks.

"Yes. Sorry. What'd you find?"

"It's Alprazolam. Medication against psychological problems. Anxiety."

"So is Derrick crazy?"

"No, of course not. Stop that. You're not crazy, Marie. You're just having a hard time right now is all."

I feel my skin tight against me, and my lungs are empty and deflated. A sinking feeling of dread hangs over, and then crashes against me in a terrible, heavy torrent. I feel like I can barely stand.

"Who's Marie?" I mumble.

"M.?" Liam says over the phone.

I hang up.

I go out into the street and my breath returns to me a little. From where I stand I can see the billboard going up on 23rd and Garden. It's nearly complete. All that remains is for them to give the pants-suited body that's depicted a face—my face. I don't know why, but I get the urge to stand there on the curb, waiting for them to finish it. I'd wait as long as I'd have to. I want to see my face. That would bring me comfort somehow.

I start to walk and I find myself on Tall Grass Place. I remember the address on the bottle of pills and decide to pay Dr. Braxton's office a visit. I have no idea what I intend to find there, or even if it exists. I only know that I have to go. I've known I'd have to go all along, but I've put it off until this moment. I walk up to the building—1234—and I wonder why. I wonder why now when I've put it off for so long.

The building is small—no bigger than a residential home—and sits between two enormous brownstone apartment buildings that cast long, dark shadows on it. Despite this, I can clearly read the faded bronze plaque to the right of the door.

DR. BRAXTON PARKER, M.D.

I take a deep breath and walk inside.

The door opens into a sort of waiting room. A row of chairs sits along the far wall, and a single coffee table stands in the center stacked nearly three feet high with magazines. I walk over to them and begin to rifle through the pile. Strangely, they're all literary magazines—anthologies containing short fiction or editorials reviewing new novels and collections by up and coming writers. Some of the faces I recognize—H. T. Derr for one—but some I don't. As I go through the pile I realize that I haven't seen a single one that even mentions me. This sets off my nerves a little, but I keep them in check. I know there has to be at least one that talks about *Hard Times in a Small Town*.

I flip through the pile—faster now and growing more frantic by the second—trying to find even a tangential reference to my book. I scan the interviews, knowing that someone must have brought me up in discussing their own writing. I scan the critiques, thinking that one of them had to have thought that my depiction of small town charm was far superior than the one in some new novel—some new novel that wasn't a #1 Best Seller.

"Are you looking for something in particular?" a woman's voice asks, but I don't look up. I don't answer it.

I hear someone walking towards me, but I'm almost at the bottom of the pile. There's only a few more.

"Ma'am, can I get you to fill this out?" the voice asks, and I think I recognize it, but I'm nearly at the bottom. Two more.

"Ma'am?" she says again and I recognize her as soon as I've reached the bottom of the pile. I begin to tremble and my legs give out from under me. The woman—the blonde woman in the car with the beehive hairdo—catches me and I stare at the black book in my hand that was at the bottom of the pile of magazines.

"You alright?" the woman asks.

I open the book and flip through the pages. At first I'm relieved—it's not blank—but my relief turns to horror as I read the first line.

A #1 BEST SELLER BY
M. L. LEKESY

I read the second and third lines, scanning all the way down the page. They all say the same thing. Every page says the same thing.

"Could you fill this out please?" the woman asks, handing me a clipboard. I look up at her and down to the paper clipped to it. It's already filled out for me.

I'm gasping for breath, but I manage to speak when I look at the first line. "My name's not Marie."

The woman takes the clipboard from me and gives me a condescending smile.

"There's something wrong with it," I say, and I realize that there's something wrong with everything.

"Something wrong, Miss Kelsey?" a man says, walking through a door in front of me. He has a white lab coat and a stethoscope around his neck. "Are you ready?"

I nod and pick myself up off the floor as the blonde receptionist with the beehive hairdo hands him the clipboard. He looks at it and his face grows cold and serious. He nods to her and hands it back. When he looks back to me, his coldness has passed. He's warm and inviting and smiling.

"Are we ready, Miss Lekesy?"

I follow him through the door and down a long hallway. I'm expecting to see a desk or other rooms coming off of it, but there's only a single door at the far end. He opens it and ushers me inside. He flips on a light and motions for me to take a seat on an examination table that sits in the right corner of the small room. I do, and notice a row of ceiling-mounted cabinets—faux wood—that hang above the swivel chair he sits down in. The room is strangely empty.

He takes a pair of eyeglasses out from his shirt

pocket and puts them on, squinting as he looks at a piece of paper he's pulled out of his coat pocket. He stares at it for a long time.

"Dr. Braxton?" I say at last.

"Yeah," he replies, looking up from the wad of paper.

"Is the prescription Derrick's?"

"What's it say on the bottle?"

"It says it is."

"Then I guess it is," he says, and goes back to his paper.

I watch him, and then blurt out, "I think something's wrong with me."

He looks up slowly. "What kind of something?"

"I don't know."

He stares at me, leaning forward in his swivel chair. "I think you do."

"No, I don't." I don't know what else to say, but he just stares at me so I feel like I have to say something, even if I don't have the words to convey it. "I just feel like everything's wrong somehow. I feel wrong. I don't feel like a person. I feel like a ghost—something ethereal—flitting in and out of existence. I pop in to sign my name on a piece of paper and blink out just as quickly as I came."

He stares, and slowly crumples up the paper in his hand, letting it fall to the ground. Without saying a word, he gets up from his chair and walks out of the room, closing the door behind him.

I slide off the examination table and walk to the piece of paper, consumed with a sick sense of curiosity that makes me feel as if my stomach is full of rocks. I know I have to, so I pick it up and spread it out on the cushion of the chair. I recognize the handwriting immediately—from the dream—the nightmare.

BENJAMIN WAS A GOOD SON, I ONLY WISH HE COULD HAVE LIVED TO BECOME A GOOD MAN. I WISH I COULD'VE SEEN HIM BRING HOME A GIRL. I WISH I COULD'VE SEEN HIM GET MARRIED. HAVE CHILDREN. I WISH HE WAS HERE TODAY—EVEN IF ONLY FOR TODAY. I'D HOLD HIM ONE MORE TIME, AND I WOULDN'T COMPLAIN IF HE CRIED THE WHOLE TIME. I WOULD LET HIM CRY, BECAUSE AT LEAST I COULD HEAR HIM. AT LEAST HE'D BE HERE.

My head is heavy and it's like I'm drunk. I can barely see as I open the door and stumble back down the hall. The flames are converging from my peripherals, and Benjy is wailing—burning in his crib. My father is downstairs, practicing his eulogy.

"Benjamin was a good son…"

When I get to the waiting room, the woman with the beehive hairdo runs up to me. She looks concerned, but I can't hear what she's saying.

"I wish he were here today—even if only for today."

I rush out the door and onto the street. I run down Tall Grass Place and onto Garden Street. I'm a woman possessed, and I feel as if I'll die if I don't see it. It's the only thing that can save me. I go on and suddenly I'm in front of it. The billboard. I read the bold letters and my heart calms. Even more, I look up at my face smiling back at me—the sign is complete—holding my book, my creation. I smile, and I assume it must look like that smile—the smile the giant me is giving to all the city's occupants. She's smiling and holding her creation, her #1 Best Seller.

I'm happy knowing she's me.

I'm sitting in the passenger's seat of Derrick's car as we speed through the city. It's an early Friday morning, and my flight for Sweden leaves in two hours. Despite my excitement, I barely say a word. I think Derrick finds this odd because he keeps looking over to me as he drives.

"Watch out, honey," I say, pointing to the road ahead. He's making me nervous.

"I'm fine. I'm fine," he says, but he still keeps looking at me. "Are you fine?"

"Yeah. I'm just nervous about the flight."

"Don't be," he laughs. "I can't believe it. This time tomorrow I'll be dating a Nobel Prize winner."

I smile, but I don't feel at ease. I will tomorrow.

When I hold the prize in my hand and give my speech and hear the applause. Then I'll be happy. Until then, I'll be cautious. I can't help but feel that it's too good to be true—that the rug will slide out from under me if I get too excited. I know that's ridiculous.

We turn onto the freeway and the road makes a steep incline. We follow it higher and higher and I can see the whole city below me. Peeking from behind one of the buildings is the billboard. I watch it as we drive on, but it's strange. It seems to follow me, like the moon on a clear night. I stare at it as disappears behind a multi-story apartment complex. I turn back around, seeing it's reflection in the rear-view mirror. I can barely believe my eyes. Its supports are enormous now, and it looms high over the building. It's the tallest thing in the city skyline.

"Derrick," I say, worry plaguing my voice, "look in the mirror."

"What?" he says.

"Look at the billboard."

He cranes his neck, trying to see from my angle. "I can't see anything, honey. I'm trying to drive."

"Okay." I stare at the reflection, and I think I see it growing taller.

When we get to the airport he drops me off at the curb and goes to the trunk to get my suitcase. I can't see the billboard anymore, just its steel supports. The rest is obscured by the clouds.

"Do you see that?" I ask him, pointing.

He puts down my suitcase and squints. "Oh, yeah! That's your billboard, right? They put it up quick."

He walks over to me and kisses my cheek. "Have a good flight, babe. I want to hear all about it when you get back."

"Okay," I answer.

I make it to my gate with time to spare, so I get a coffee and think about a sequel for *Hard Times in a Small Town*. My mind is blank. The only thing that comes to me is Dr. Braxton. Maybe I could do a spin off focusing on Dr. Braxton? Maybe not.

The stewardess announces the first boarding call so I get up and walk to the desk and show her my first-class ticket. She scans it and I walk onto the catwalk. It's dark, and for some reason the floor lights aren't on. I get in the line and, slowly, we shamble into the plane.

I seat myself by the window and get comfortable, hoping that no one sits next to me. I don't feel like talking. I'm relieved when they close the doors. The stewardess walks over to the intercom and begins her safety spiel while I put in my headphones and try to drown her out.

After we take off and the fasten seatbelt light goes off, I unbuckle my seatbelt and stretch my legs. I feel like a drink—maybe a mimosa—so I gently tap the side of one of the stewardesses as she passes. She turns around and looks at me and I shrink back into my seat in surprise.

"Yes?" the brunette with the beehive asks.

"It's you," I say. The words just come out.

"Pardon?"

"Um, could I get a mimosa?"

"Certainly," she says and hurries off to the back of the plane.

I'm shaking, but I try to calm down. I'm probably just overtired. I switch off my music and take out my sleeping mask and neck pillow, intent on getting some rest. Almost as soon as I do someone rushes over and takes the seat next to mine.

"I hope you don't mind, luv, there's a baby wailing up a storm back there," he says. I know who it is. I tear off my mask and see the man with the leather trilby.

"Ya miss me, luv?" he says.

"Who are you?"

"Keep your fucking voice down. There's no need for hysterics."

"Who are you?"

He smiles. "Who are you? That's the question you should be asking."

The attendant, the brunette with the beehive, comes back my way and attempts to hand me the mimosa.

"I'll take that, luv. Thanks," the man says. He grabs it out of her hand and drains it in one gulp before looking at me. "Helps to calm the nerves, don't it?"

I don't say anything in response. I just look at him.

"C'mon, luv. You couldn't have expected this ride to go on forever. This silliness has gone on for long enough already."

The captain's voice crackles over the speakers.

"Attention passengers, this is your captain. I'm turning the fasten seat belt light back on. Everyone needs to please return to their seats and remain calm."

"Remain calm?" I say to no one.

The man in the trilby smirks and tightens his seatbelt. "This is it, Marie. End of the road—or jet stream or whatever."

A feeling of panic spreads through the cabin of the plane. Women are muttering. The men are looking around frantically, tugging at the skirts of the flight attendants and asking them a multitude of questions.

"What's happening?" I ask the man in the trilby.

He lowers his hat down over his eyes and sinks down into his chair, completely relaxed. "Just sit back and enjoy the flight, luv."

"Oh my God!" someone shouts.

The entire plane rushes to the windows, pressing their faces on the glass. The man in the row ahead of me shouts, "What the fuck is that?" I don't look at first, but as the seconds tick by I slowly lean towards the window and look out.

I don't see anything—only the clouds and the blue sky—but, slowly, an object slides into view from the nose of the plane. It's enormous and incredibly close. The sun reflects off its two steel poles, and I can make out the words, "#1 Best Seller."

"Is that a billboard?" the man asks.

"Sure looks like it," someone answers.

"Who's it of?" asks a woman.

"We're headed right for it!"

I'm overwhelmed with emotion, but one bubbles to the surface more prominently than all the others. I unbuckle my seatbelt and stand up.

"It's me!" I shout over the cries of the passengers. "I'm M. L. Lekesy. My book, *Hard Times in a Small Town* is a work of genius, a literary achievement crafted by a unique and intelligent voice that truly speaks to the marvels—and the horrors—of the human condition."

No one's listening, but the man in the trilby laughs. "You tell 'em, luv."

A tremendous crash and suddenly I'm hurling through the sky. I can see the plane above me. Its left wing is falling aimlessly at its side, and has taken part of the fuselage along with it. Everything is fire and I'm reminded of the dream. I can see the billboard clear and intact—the enormous me in the sky smiling down.

"You're one lucky bitch."

"Excuse me?" I say. I don't know this one. The store goes through so many employees it's difficult to keep everyone straight. That, and I've missed so many days.

"You check out for two weeks and just come waltzing back in here all hunky dory? You're a lucky bitch. I'd have fired your ass."

"Well, I guess I'm lucky you're not my boss," I snap back. I don't know who this woman thinks she is. Her name tag says Alicia, but I think "asshole" would be more accurate.

She rolls her eyes with a huff. "Damn right you're lucky." As she walks back into the store, she stops at a rack of men's jeans. I guess she works in Men's.

It's been three days since everything and it's been ten days since I've gone to work at Greenburt's. Nothing seems to have changed. The people still come and go—mostly just browsers—and the employees still talk amongst themselves and stare at their phones until Mr. Neaves comes and yells at them to fold something. The browsers really do a number on the displays.

In all actuality, though, I really am lucky. I'm sure the city is just bursting with unskilled workers who could learn to run a register and put up a coat display in about ten minutes flat. Mr. Neaves is really doing me a solid, and I'm not entirely sure why. Maybe he's just lazy and doesn't want to do the paperwork.

I should feel grateful, but the only thing I feel is

nerves. My entire body is one giant pulsating electrical signal, making me jump at everything and everyone. The sadness went out a while ago, but I'm sure it'll be back. It'll come back when I'm in the shower or going to the laundromat—I need to do laundry soon. But not yet. Not until this first primary feeling is gone—this feeling that keeps me up all night hearing sirens in my sleep. The oldest one there is: Self-preservation and Darwin and all that, coupled with some Grade-A Raskalnikov shit. Maybe it will go away soon. I just hope that, when it does, it's not accompanied by a pair of handcuffs.

I still don't know if Chuck is alive. But I'm not thinking. I'm just staring at the Men's department as Mr. Neaves walks up to the register I'm on, panting heavily. He's a big guy. I study his face, thinking that maybe my luck has worn out. He looks annoyed, but, then again, he always looks annoyed.

"You've got a call," he says. "It's in the back. It's on some kinda timer or something. You better hurry."

I leave the register and walk past Alicia, who just glares at me. She was probably watching—hoping that Neaves was telling me to go the hell home. Not today at least. I've got a little while yet.

The only phone outside of the one in Mr. Neaves' office hangs on the plain, unfinished concrete wall next to the time clock. One of the other cashiers is standing next to it, waiting the two minutes until 3:00 when she's supposed to clock out. There's a green solid light next to the words "Line 1." I put my back to the girl, hit the button, and pick up the phone.

It's Chuck and he starts talking almost immediately. "Are you there now? You there?"

A wave of emotion courses through me, drawing out water from my eyes. I didn't know this about myself. I didn't know I cared. Maybe I shouldn't. Maybe I don't actually. Maybe I'm just stressed out. "Chuck! I didn't know what happened I—"

"W-we can't talk—" he whispers, his voice barely audible, "not here on the phone."

"But you called me."

"I know. They're moving me all around. I—" he stops. There's another voice with him, a deeper one, mumbling in the background. Chuck's breath goes shallow, and he talks in a low, dull voice I can hardly hear. I can't hear. All I can make out are the words, "Bad" and "Something else."

"Chuck, you have to speak up. I can't hear you."

The line is dead and moaning a dull, electronic tone. A computer woman's voice chimes, "The inmate has ended the call."

Inmate? So they got him, then. Of course they did. I don't know what I was expecting. He was unconscious or dazed or something in the back seat of an overturned car. They were right behind us. There was no chance at all. At least he's alive. At least there's that.

As I walk back to the register, the knowledge sinks in—as do the implications. He's told them everything. He's not the type to keep it all in. No one is. Even gangsters get a stipend for silence—money to their families or something. Chuck's getting nothing—nothing but multiple life-sentences hanging over his head, I'm sure. Of course they found the bodies. And of course he told them everything. He told them about me. Maybe that's why he sounded so out of it on the phone. He was sorry.

I walk back to the counter where Mr. Neaves is watching my register. I look him in the face and say, "I quit."

He's taken aback. "You're quitting? Now?"

"I have to." I don't wait for another word. I take off my nametag, lay it on the desk, and walk out of the store. There's no time for thinking.

I do a line behind my purse in the subway train. It turns out there was a little more than just over the counter stuff in that medicine cabinet. A couple of pricey prescriptions. I was just too frazzled to notice. The smoke bottle could have gotten me a lot more money if it hadn't been too hot to touch.

People used to say I was good with words. When I was really little Dad would sneak into my room and read my diary when I wasn't looking. I'd get mad, of course, but he'd say he wasn't being nosy, he just liked reading it. Said it was like poetry. I don't know how true that is, but it's a nice memory from before. He stopped reading when I got older and I hid it in my underwear drawer.

When Jim said it, I'm sure he wasn't being pandering. He knew what he was talking about. He read all kinds of stuff—classics, horror, sci-fi, comic books. If it had words he had already read it, was currently reading it, or he knew about it and was going to read it right after this thing he was reading now.

He didn't say my writing was like poetry, he said it was like music. Said he could hear the words being spoken—like an actual voice, beautiful and strange—and they all flowed and rumbled and rolled together in a kind of rich tapestry of sound and meaning. That was the way he talked—some redneck boy from Alabama...

I stick the tiny plastic bag of white back into my purse. It's my entire net-worth at this point.

The train grinds to a halt and I get off at Derringer Street. It's about 5:30 in the evening. It's Thursday so I know Bill isn't at his apartment. He's drinking at Stein's—that's my bet. It's like an Irish pub, but without the Irish and a lot bigger—a glowing pink neon sign. It's just a short walk.

When I get there, I walk into the bar and I see him. He's sitting in a booth with a couple of his work friends. I don't recognize them. He makes eye contact with me, but then looks quickly away. I sit down next to him, and he scoots over awkwardly.

"Haven't seen you in a while," he says, looking at his friends nervously. They look confused.

"This your wife?" one of them asks, a much younger one with black hair gelled to the side.

I look at Bill. He gives a wry smile and puts his

arm around me, squeezing. "Yep, this is her," he says. "Ain't she a cutie?"

The two other men look at each other awkwardly, but eventually agree. One of their friends shows up—a kid even younger than them who looks straight out of college—and they order more beer and get loud on the other side of the table. Bill drains his glass and orders a shot of whiskey before turning to me.

"What the fuck are you doing here?" he whispers. "Doris will murder you if she finds out."

I kiss him on the neck. He tastes like old man cologne and sweat. "I need money, and a place to stay."

He smiles, and shakes his head slowly from side to side. "And this being a capitalist society...you're taking that into account, right? Payment for goods rendered?"

I slide my hand across his legs, and clamp down between—hard but not too hard.

"Well, alright then..."

We leave the table and I blow him in the bathroom. "Just like old times," he says. It takes him a while, which is not like old times at all.

He puts back on his pants and opens up his wallet. "I've got a buddy who owns a hotel downtown. They're not doing too well, so he'll put you up cheap. The Hotel Longhorn." He hands me $100 and a scrap of paper. It's a phone number.

"I don't have a phone," I say.

"Just hold onto it. That's not the hotel. It's something else. Somebody's been looking for you—

calling me day and night. I don't really know why I kept the number. Maybe I thought I might run into you eventually. Maybe you get your next hundo from him, eh?"

I look up from the paper and he's out of the stall, his shoes clacking on the tile. I'm alone. I do a quick line and step out of the bathroom. The bar is filling up, but I don't see Bill anywhere. His coworkers are still laughing and hollering amongst themselves.

Sure, Bill paid and everything, but something was different about him. He had a sadness to him that wasn't there before when it was all fire and lust and flesh. It was like he was doing it out of sympathy. But who's ever heard of that? It was strange. I think his well is running dry.

I go up to the bar and order a beer and Scotch. I'm starting to feel a lot better. I take the Scotch in one shot, and, as I sip my beer, I stare at the numbers on the scrap of paper. I guess I have to call it. I have no choice in the matter. It could be Chuck, but Bill knows Chuck. At least, knows of him. He used to always tease me about my "boyfriend" back when our business together was more regular. He would have said "Chuck," not "Somebody." If it's not Chuck I don't know who it is, and not knowing isn't an option.

That's what this number is. It's just another one—another guy with money and a dick.

"You want another?" the bartender asks, taking my empty glass.

"Yeah, do you have a phone?"

He reaches below the bar and produces a shiny black corded telephone, placing it in front of me. "You need a cab?"

"No, I need a phone," I say, picking up the receiver and dialing the number on the paper. As it rings, the entire bar goes quiet. Maybe only in my mind or maybe the ringing is louder than normal. It's all I hear. The electronic chirp of the bells.

"Hello?" the voice says on the other end, reaching back—back beyond the smoking bottle and cloud and the city. It's transcending all that and tugging at some long—forgotten string buried deep in the red muscle of my chest. The voice is different—deeper—but somehow exactly the same.

"Jim?" I say, a knot forming in the back of my throat—rising, hardening.

"I can't hear anything," he says. "Who is this?"

It's the noise of the bar and I hadn't even noticed. I lower my head, and cup the receiver with the other hand.

"Jim?" I say again. The name warbles out, betraying all the pent up history of the last twelve years.

"Marie?" he says, and in the way he used to say it when the sun was brighter. "Is that you?"

I'm nodding yes because the word isn't coming. "Yes," I say at last, stifling a mix of laughter and sobs.

"It's been years. I've been trying to get in touch with you."

The diner and the touch of his hand on mine. "I've been here—just really busy," I say. It's the only thing I think of—the only thing to account for the years of waste.

"Why'd you call? Why now?"

"I got your number."

"It hasn't changed. You know I got the house when my dad died. You've had it this whole time."

I stare at the numbers on the paper. I do recognize them. Why hadn't I before? I had called this number hundreds of times—the lines connected, sending tiny sparks of electricity and sound back and forth for hours and well into the night. Laughter and jokes and, sometimes, other things...

"This is a business phone, miss," the bartender says. He's standing over me, peering down.

"I'll just be a second," I say. He rolls his eyes and goes to help a woman with another martini.

"Why didn't you call before? I left you a ton of messages. Samantha gave me your number."

"I don't have a phone."

"Oh, I thought—"

"Now, miss!" the bartender shouts from the other end. He's walking this way.

"Listen," I interrupt, "I'm staying at a hotel. I'll call you when I get there, okay?"

"Oh, okay."

"You'll be there, right? You're available?"

The bartender hits the hook and the line goes dead. I want to leap over the bar and gouge his fucking eyes out, but I smile and get up slowly. As I walk away, I hear him call after me "Miss, you didn't pay! Hello!?!" but I'm already out the door.

As I walk to the subway it hits me. Jim Bridges. I just talked with Jim Bridges for the first time in twelve years. The fact is strange—surreal to me—and I don't know how to feel. All my feelings are mixed up and muddled. It's getting dark.

I can't call him again. I shouldn't have the first time and I wouldn't have if I had known—if I had remembered. I think I had known. I think I did recognize the number when Bill handed it to me, but I called it anyway. Why? Why did I want to get close to the fire again? That fire. That fire's been sending its smoke cloud after me ever since...and I called its phone number. I'm inching closer and closer and soon I'll be burned. Not just burned. Consumed—my skin black and ash. Like Benjamin's...

I'm holding the paper, but I crumple it up and shove it back in my pocket. I pass several trashcans. I don't throw it away.

·· ·· ·· ·· ·· ·· ·· ··

I get to the hotel a little before 9:00. It's an ancient place, but not ancient like the buildings that surround the park. Those are well kept, and feel more like museums than century-old buildings. The Hotel Longhorn shows age itself—bearing time's slow erosion on its every crack and with every fleck of chipped paint. It's a shit-hole.

Passing through the door to the lobby, I notice that the interior isn't much better—tacky, floral wallpaper and beige carpets. There's an old man at the counter, and he shoots up when he sees me.

"Welcome to the Hotel Longhorn. How may I serve you?" he says, a slight warble in his voice. His eyes are pleasant.

"Hey." I walk up to the counter. "I'm friends with Bill Byer. He said you could get me a room."

He leans over the counter and studies me—up and down. "No bags? It's unusual for someone to come to a hotel with no bags."

"I've got what I need on me."

"I can see that," he smiles, and then begins furiously typing into the computer. "How long will you be staying with us?"

"I don't know yet."

"Don't know?"

"Not yet."

"Hmmm," he says, and his face darkens. His brow furrows and his eyes seem to subtly vibrate in their sockets. "Will you be having any guests?"

"No. Just me."

"No lovers, then?"

His eyes aren't pleasant anymore. I take a deep breath. "Look, how much for the fucking room?"

He reaches down below the desk, brings out a keycard and a scrap of paper, and hands both to me. "We'll settle up later. Enjoy your stay!"

I look at the paper. It's blank. All white. "What's the room number?"

"It's the top floor. Once you get out of the elevator, take a right and it's the fourth door on the left."

I nod dumbly and head to the elevator. I hit the

button. It glows. Tatar Heights. Phil dancing around my brain with his solid-black card, swiping at key pads that unlock yet more doors leading into more burning rooms. Jim's inside one of the rooms saying why didn't you call before? I left you a ton of messages...

With a ding, the elevator doors open. I step inside and hit the glowing number "8." The light above me shines down.

When I get to the floor, I take a right and then walk up to the fourth door on the left—just like the man told me to. There are numbers affixed to the wood of every other door, but there aren't any on this one. Just a large white splotch of paint where a number might have been—a perfect match to the empty white paper I'm holding.

I put the card up to the keypad and it beeps acceptingly. The lock disengages with a satisfying clang and I walk inside the room, fumbling along the wall closest to me for a light switch. I find it, and flip it on. A single lamp that sits on a night table illuminates the room faintly in dull yellow. It's the only light I see.

The room is sparse—very sparse. A bed, a night stand, and a desk against the wall. Not even a TV. But compared to what I'm used to with Chuck, it's a huge step up. The only issue is that this filth isn't known filth. It's a collective filth—years upon years of strangers' bodies that's sunk into every fiber and every molecule of the place. Everything moist and vaporous and smelling just a little like wet dog. But it's home now. I don't know for how long.

I take off my shoes, throw them by the door, and light up a cigarette before collapsing onto the bed. I close my eyes, but I don't sleep. Faces pass before and over me. First Chuck's, then Jim's, and then Phil's—his bearing that strange sarcastic half-smile and shooting bullets out of his eyes that blow up the other two. I do a quick line on the nightstand. I'll call him, Jim. It's been such a long time. Such a long time...

I dial the number and the phone starts to ring like an alarm in my head. I hang up, slamming it down on the hook.

I do another line. I think that it'll keep me up, but my eyes start to sag. Maybe it's already been hours. I lay my head down for just a second, but I'm gone.

It's still dark out. The only light that passes through the thick curtains over the window is faint, its color alternating in reds and blues and yellows from the life outside. Why am I awake? There's someone banging on my door.

"I don't need anything," I shout, thinking it must be room service. I look at the clock on the nightstand. It's 3:33. Definitely not room service.

The banging stops for a moment, but then resumes louder and more forceful than before. I wrap the sheets around my body tight, hoping the noise will go away. It doesn't.

"Miss Kelsey," a voice says through the door,

muffled by the wood. It's deep and monotone. "I'm coming in now."

The door chimes and the lock slams open. I sit up in bed, my eyes fixed on the doorway as a tall man in a black suit and tie enters. On his lapel, he has the pin of a gray dove. He puts it away quickly, but I still see it. I see as he slips it into his right pocket—a solid black card, just like Phil's.

"Good morning, Miss Kelsey," the man says. His voice booming—loud. He stands at attention with his hands behind his back.

The fear is there—real, trembling. "What do you want? How do you know my name?"

"I come on behalf of Charles," he says. "He wants to speak with you."

"Charles?"

"Chuck."

"Chuck..." The word hangs in the air. I don't understand what's going on. "Who are you?"

The man smirks. "Get dressed, Miss Kelsey. We're leaving."

I can see it in my head—all of it. Him taking me somewhere and me never coming back—never going anywhere again. "And and what if I don't want to go with you?"

The man walks over to the bathroom door, still smirking. "Have you showered yet?"

I don't answer, and he motions for me to come to him. Cautiously, I get out of the bed and walk over, still wearing my clothes from the day before. His smirk shrinks, and he slowly raises his index finger, pointing to the bathroom door.

"Open it," he says.

I nod and slowly push the door open. It's dark as pitch. I can't see a thing—just shimmering shapes that dance and swirl, played strangely by the scant light that bounces off the bathroom mirror.

He points to the hot water knob on the shower. "Turn it."

"Why?" I ask. "What will happen?"

His finger hangs in the air, wavering slightly. "Turn it."

The tile is cold on my bare feet as I walk to the shower, the curtain shimmering in the light breeze coming from the air vent. I grasp the knob and look back to the man. I don't know what's happening. I don't...

"Turn it," he says again.

Slowly, I begin to turn and the knob begins to give. All at once a huge column of flame erupts from the shower head with an enormous crash, shooting red-hot chrome, metal, and drywall everywhere and turning the previously dark room into a burning ball of light. I have no time to react. I just stare dumbly as I'm thrown aside, tossed out of the shower and onto the carpet behind the bathroom. It happens so fast—so incredibly fast. The man overtop of me, shielding me from the blast.

As the dust and debris slowly settles, he picks himself off the ground and dusts off his pants. He's completely unharmed.

My eyes bulging. "Thank you," I gasp, the wind barely returning to my lungs. "How did you—"

He looks down and offers me his hand. "Thank Chuck." He lifts me to my feet and speaks in short, loud bursts. "Get dressed, Miss Kelsey. We're leaving."

"But where are we going?"

"Out."

"I don't have any clothes with me. They're at the apartment." The robbery and the bodies and the crash and the police bear down on me like a hurricane.

"Hmmm," he says, and walks to the door. He opens it and motions for me to walk through. "We're leaving."

I put on my shoes and we walk down to the street and to a black luxury sedan parked nearby. My senses are on high-alert and I'm scanning, searching, noting—looking for anything and any way that I can get out. He opens the rear passenger door for me, and I climb in as he shuts it with a loud clang. Isolated in that strange car, the reality of my situation hits me. It hits me harder as the man starts the car and drives away. I'm being kidnapped, and I was almost killed by a bomb hidden in my hotel room shower.

"You can get another room," the man says, looking straight ahead at the empty city road.

I don't answer—not immediately. I have to cooperate, at least for now, but I also need to know. "Did you plant it, the bomb?" I ask.

"No. That's not how I work," he says, his eyes glaring in the mirror. "That's not how any of this works."

It's growing now—coming full force. I feel it all over—sliding under my skin and under my fingernails, burning and ripping. "What do you want with me?" I ask, my voice nothing but a swollen lump.

"Please be quiet, Miss Kelsey," the man replies. "I'm trying to drive."

I don't say another word.

We leave the city, flying over the bridge and the water, and we keep going—past the suburbs and the shopping malls, past the highways of nothing. We drive even when the road turns to dirt, too narrow for more than one car at a time and flanked on all sides by tall dry grass. Tall grass. I recognize it. I know that somewhere nestled in that sea of grass is a clearing that holds a little Dutch Colonial-style house. If I could see it, maybe I would see a little girl peeking out through the windows, waving at the little boy with the accent who's walking up the dirt road to meet her...

It's been hours, but he finally stops in the middle of the road just as the sun begins to rise.

"We're here," he says.

"Where's here?"

"Stay in the car." He gets out, closes the door behind him, and stands at attention in front of the car.

I look through my window. There can't be anything for miles except dry, burned grass. No one can hear me. No one can help. The grass blows gently in the wind, but one patch isn't. It's jolting, moving violently from side to side as if some great animal was running and weaving through, chasing after its prey. As I look I can see that the motion is drawing nearer, pushing even closer stalks aside—drawing closer and closer to the car. Then a bit of hair. Then a face.

"Let me in! Let me in! Let me in!" Chuck screams, his voice raw and haggard, banging on the car window.

The man in the suit walks to my door and opens it. Chuck barrels into the car, and I slide to the side as he closes it behind him.

"Chuck, what—"

He cuts me off. "There's no time. I need to get back. I needed to see you, to warn you." He's wearing a bright orange jumpsuit with the black number 333 emblazoned on the chest.

"Why couldn't you call?"

"No good. He's tracking everything. He's imbedded." He gnashes his teeth. "Deeply imbedded. He's in fucking everything. Fucking everywhere. It was a mistake to get him involved. A goddamn mistake."

"Mr. Hammon," the black-suited man says from beyond the car door. "Please try to keep calm. Think of your heart."

"What's wrong with your heart?"

"Nothing. Not important. You need to stay away from him. Get out. He's not going to stop. Never."

"Who?"

"Phil. He's gunning for me—for us. He's afraid—not for the robbery. Something else.

Something we both did before. He's afraid I told you something." He's scared, more scared than I've ever seen him before. "He put something in my food. My chest is on fire."

"Mr. Hammon," the man says, tapping on the window.

"I've got to go," Chuck says, "I've got to get back. Just get out of here, and stay away from Phil, alright? I love you."

I don't say it back. I just stare as he runs off—back into the grass he had emerged from before.

The man climbs back into the car and starts it up. He turns the car around and we head back the way we came. I don't say anything for a long time, and he seems okay with the silence. My mind's a blur with shower-head bombs and decapitations and shootings and who knows what else—there are plenty of terrible ways to die. I don't know if I can believe Chuck, but I have no reason not to. That, and his expression was too real. He was shaking, and his voice wasn't his. It wasn't the Chuck I knew. It was a Chuck in the grips of an unadulterated, unspeakable fear. I'm catching it now, too. I don't have any money. I don't have anything. I'm defenseless. I'll be dead within a week. I know it. I can see myself lying in the gutter—eyes unblinking with blood running out my chest. I'm dead, and for what? For a brick of coke that we never even had. God I need a hit. I need something to calm me down. The thoughts are buzzing like flies—loud and swerving—and I need something to calm them down. I need to think.

It's bubbling up. I can't contain it anymore. As soon as we get onto the highway, I blurt it out, all my fear and rage directed at those eyes in the rearview mirror. "Are you going to help me? Is that why you're here?"

The man is expressionless. "Charles was good to us, so we're being good to him. He needed to see you, and we could make the arrangement. What happens now is not our concern. We've got plenty of more concerning concerns."

I can tell there's no room for argument and my left hand is shaking. I need to make a call.

We get back in the city and it's almost 9:00 in the morning. We drive over the bridge and into downtown, and we stop outside the Hotel Longhorn.

"You can't be serious," I say.

The man turns toward me. "Why can't I be?"

My voice dampens. "He knows where I am. He blew up my bathroom. I can't go back here."

"You can get another room."

"In the same hotel?"

He slowly points up to the eighth floor, his hand wavering in the air. "Look under your pillow."

"What?"

His hand is still there. "When you get back to your room, look under your pillow."

"I don't under—"

He raises his voice—loud as thunder, but still just as monotone. "It's time for you to leave, Miss Kelsey."

I get out of the car and he speeds off, flying

through the intersection and taking a hard left at the next. I'm left alone, standing on the sidewalk outside the hotel.

"Miss, miss!" the old desk clerk calls out—the same one as before. He's holding the door for me, beckoning me inside with a wave of his bony, withered hand. "So sorry about this morning. It's the damned water pressure." He looks around, surprised and nervous, and then repeats in a whisper, "The damned water pressure. It was entirely too high. We're real sorry about that. I have no idea how it got that way. It must have been pretty powerful—to come shooting off the base like that! It's a miracle you weren't hurt."

"What? What water pressure?"

His eyes grow wide. "You weren't hurt, were you?"

"No, but it wasn't water pressure." It wasn't water pressure. "Why do you think it was water pressure?"

The man's embarrassed—maybe annoyed. "Well, that's what the cleaning woman told me. I haven't been up there myself. We had maintenance replace it. He fixed the pressure too, and we're happy to cover the rest of your stay here—free, of course."

"It wasn't water pressure. The thing exploded."

"And we have replaced it," he says curtly. He walks back to the desk, smiling.

What water pressure? My feet are as heavy as lead but I have to go. I have to find out.

I pass through the lobby and ride the elevator

up to the eighth floor. I get to my room—the room with the white splotch on the door—and walk inside, half expecting to see Phil grinning with a steak knife in his hand. I think I do see him, but it's not him. It's something else. It's a thin, pale thing with long fingers that drag the floor, cowering—no—crouching in the tall grass.

It's not there. He's not there. The room's untouched—intact. There's no smell of charred metal like before—just the lemon-fresh scent of cleaner. I open the door to the bathroom. It's all there. No busted walls, shattered porcelain, or drywall dust coating the surfaces. There's nothing—nothing but a shiny new shower head gleaming in the fluorescent light.

It's not possible. I had seen the carnage myself. The room destroyed—decimated by a fiery explosion that I only barely escaped from. But the man in the suit was fine...He hadn't been hurt. Neither of us were.

I tilt my head as if it will give me an answer. Was there really no explosion? Was it my own imagination—that same smoke and fire from before—coming back to me, inserting itself violently into my here and now? It wouldn't be the first time, but it had been content to mostly occupy only that small corner of my brain until now—that small sharp corner that punctures and thrusts into all the others. The pill bottle and the shower head.

There's an uneasy feeling growing in the pit of my stomach. I call the front desk and ask for a different room. The clerk says he'll check the bookings and call me back. The bookings. I haven't seen another soul in this place.

I sit down on the bed. If Phil is going to kill me he's going to kill me sooner rather than later. He knows I'll be lying low from Tatar Heights—or maybe he thinks I skipped town. Maybe he'll give me some time, thinking I'll just waltz into our apartment when the heat's died down. But he knows I don't have any money or means. He'll probably start his search now, and in cheap hotels—cheap hotels like this one. It won't be long. Not long at all.

I can't think anymore so I fall down onto the pillow and my head hits something hard. I reach underneath, my hand grasping cold and metal. A handgun—all black, save for the barrel that looks like polished silver. There's an inscription etched into the top: "This is the Silver-Sin Eater."

It seems to grow heavier by the second. I put it in the drawer of the nightstand and cover it with the copy of Gideons Bible.

— — — — — — — —

It's 4:00 in the afternoon and the phone is ringing. I must have been tired after the drive and the grass and Chuck in his orange jumpsuit and the bomb that maybe wasn't. I slept almost the whole day away. How? I'm being hunted, aren't I? Hunted, but I'm so tired.

My stomach is churning. I need something to eat, but first the metallic chime of the telephone bells. The desk clerk was supposed to call back with a different room for me. I pick up the phone.

"Marie, I'm here. I'm in the city," Jim's voice rings out, cutting through my sleepiness like a knife. "Where are you? Can I see you?"

My hand spasms and I drop the phone onto the bed. I can hear his distant hollow voice muttering on—faint and soft—but the louder sound is the crackling of the fire. It's falling down as ash from my nightstand, running through the carpet and slipping under my bedroom door. It's creeping quietly now through the hallway so as not to wake Mom and Dad, and then slipping underneath the door to the nursery...

"Marie? You still there?" the tiny voice calls. I answer it, picking up the phone and holding it up to my ear.

"Jim, what do you mean you're here—in the city?" I clear my throat. "How did you get this number?"

"It said I had a missed call. I figured it was you. You said you'd call me last night."

I don't answer. I can't think of anything to say.

"It's been so long. I just wanted to catch up," his voice grows somber and soft, "and I didn't want you to disappear again."

"I didn't disappear," I snap. "I've been right here the whole time."

"But I've called your phone a billion times. Did you get a new one or something?"

Yes, but no. No, it's been the same. The same the whole time. He has my number. He was the last person I called—the only one. We talked about how chickens make a weird noise when you pick them up for the last time—like they know or something. There were always chickens around the house in the tall grass. I don't have a phone.

"I don't have a phone," I say.

"Oh." He says it with an abundance of breath. I don't know if he believes me. He was always so smart. I could never get away with anything around him. I would wash my hands with dish soap over and over, and he'd still smell the smoke on my hands. I know they're bad for me, dammit. I fucking know.

"Well, I'm glad I caught you, then!" he laughs. Is it a real laugh? There's nothing funny about catching me. Maybe it's a nervous laugh, but it sounds genuine. "You hungry?"

"Yeah, but I think I'm just going to run next door."

"Don't. My treat. Where are you right now?"

"Jim..."

"Where are you? I took the bus all the way out here—I want to see you!"

There's a mirror hanging opposite the bed, and my eye catches it. I don't know what he wants to see—what he expects to see. I'm too skinny and, like he said, it's been a long time. I'm not the same as I was before—not at all—but he sounds the same. The same jilted sing-song way of talking, and the same enthusiasm pregnant in every word. It's almost too much for me. Almost...

I give it up to him. "I'm downtown. I can come

and meet you."

"I don't mind coming to you."

I look at the drawer of the nightstand. It's closed, but inside is the gun and the bible and what's left of my coke. "No, it's alright. I'll come to you. I know the trains better."

"Alright. It looks like I'm on the corner of...uh..."

I hear the sounds of the city—the cars and busses, the vendors blasting their music from their old stereos. They're all sounds I know so well. They're the soundtrack to whatever it is my life's become. And I hear Jim—Jim from before. He's among them, panting in the heat, going "uh...uh" as he squints to read the street signs.

"Looks like 14th and Geraldine," he says.

"Sounds good. I'll see you in a little," I say, and I'm smiling actually.

"I can't wait."

We say goodbye and the phone goes dead. I'm feeling jittery, but I don't open the drawer.

—————————

The smell of the lake. Water drying on my warming skin. Him warm, too. Sliding his hands along my hips and back. Kissing my neck and lips over and over until both are numb but feeling more than ever before. Him pressing and then a breaking and a bulging inside of me. Pressing and moving. Reverberating waves. The fear of being found. Guilt, but passing. Then gasping and laughing and kissing and pinching and grass against our backs and night and stars and beer on lips as well as kisses.

"I've been wanting to do that a long time," he says.

"Why didn't you?"

"I don't know." His smile shrinks, but then grows to a size bigger than before. "I guess I just didn't get the opportunity."

"Maybe you shouldn't have had it at all."

He looks at me and brings my hand to his lips. He's serious, but then the smile again and we're laughing and drinking and falling more and more into each other, pulled forward ceaselessly toward a burning star nestled somewhere out in a sky of endless possibilities—each of them good and each better than all the others combined.

Then no more stars.

With a chime the doors of the subway train open and I step out onto the platform. The stink of the city in summer has settled in deep—had all day to fester. It hits me as I mount the steps to the surface. The surface where Jim is.

I walk to the corner of 14th and Geraldine and I recognize him immediately. He's leaned up against the wall of a convenience store and messing with his phone. He's older now. He's stockier, and the lines in his face are more pronounced, but they're still the lines I remember tracing with my finger as we lay in his bed on Fridays after school—the oscillating fan blowing softly from side to side.

He doesn't see me and, for what seems like an

eternity, I only watch him. Then his name comes shooting out of my mouth like a bullet.

"Jim?"

He turns around. His face has changed. There are glasses now, thin and black-framed, and even gray patches—silver maybe—that fleck the scruff around his neck. His whole self is older, but his eyes and smile are the same.

"Marie?" He's beaming now—as infectious as ever. "It's...uh...it's been a while, huh?"

"Yeah," I laugh. We just stand there, like idiots, and with each awkward second that passes, I can't help but notice his eyes running over me up and down—noticing how thin and weak I've become, how old and tired I am, and that my teeth are yellow and my eyes buggy from too much coke.

"You alright?" His arms twinge. They were about to, but something held them back. He was about to hold me like on the lake and like at the diner but he's not. He's not because it's been a long time.

Without warning and spurred by some impulse I collide against his chest and wrap my arms around his neck, trying my best to keep the hot tears that slide down my cheek off his white button-down shirt.

"Hey..." he says, his voice soft and warm and inviting and as lovely as always, "are you alright?"

"No," I answer. "No, I'm fucking not."

He holds me for a while as the crowds pass over and around us—a wedge in a sea of people. I bury my head. I don't want to look at them. I don't want them to see us.

He kisses the top of my head. "Are you hungry? There's a pizza place around here that's got good reviews. You're supposed to get pizza in the city, right?"

I look up at him and wipe my eyes. "You can get whatever you want. There's no law saying you can only get pizza."

He smiles and presses my head back against his chest for a brief while longer. It's too brief and, when it ends, I miss the warmth. I miss hearing his heart thumping in my ears.

We walk and I can't keep my eyes off him. Now that my emotional catharsis or whatever that bastard, Dr. Braxton, would call it has come and gone, I'm left in a strange state. I don't know if he feels the same way. I just want to watch his arms wave as he walks, and his nostrils flare up as we pass a sewer grate. It's all new and exciting, but also intimate—familiar.

"You been here before?" he asks.

The sign above the door reads, "Luca's." Other than that, it doesn't look any different from the hundreds of other pizza places in the city. "I don't know. They all have the same kind of names, don't they?"

"They're all Italian, I guess."

"Or trying to be."

"Yeah. Anyway it got good reviews...unless you want to try somewhere else?"

"This is fine." I'm not really hungry for pizza. I'm not really hungry for anything—despite not having eaten all day. I'm too on edge. Having Jim here—standing next to me, our legs touching underneath the table as we slide into opposite sides of the booth, our eyes meeting over and over—is too much for me to handle. It takes all my concentration not to sprint out of the restaurant—run and keep running. That's part of me, but the other part wants to tell him everything, everything that's happened and break up the telling by touching my lips to his over and over again.

"Pepperoni good?" he asks.

"Yeah, that's fine," I answer.

The waitress takes our order and walks away into the back of the kitchen. There's a family of four eating on the other side of the restaurant, but other than that the place is pretty empty. I don't think it has good reviews.

Jim leans forward in his seat nervously, and scratches the back of his head. "So, how you been?"

"I've been alright."

"No one's heard from you in a while. I guess because you don't have a phone."

"Yeah...it broke."

"You know, if you need money, Marie..."

"No. I don't." It's definitely the same Jim. Always trying to fix everything. But there are some things you can't fix by thinking or spending money or seeing a doctor. Things can get taken away from you and never come back. He never understood that. I don't need his money. I do need his money, but it wouldn't do a lick of good. Not really.

"So, you're working, then?" he asks. I can see a

glimmer behind his eyes. Nervous. He hopes I'm working. He doesn't know if I can take care of myself—just like Mom and Dad and Sam.

"Yeah. It's a department store, but it's something. Gets me by."

"That's good. You still writing?"

I'm anxious to get the conversation off of me. "What about you? Where are you working?"

"I got dad's old auto shop. He retired about 5 years ago. Hired a couple new guys. It's going pretty well."

"He still living with you in the house?"

"Nah. He moved out and got a cabin up in the mountains. He's got service up there so we talk every once in a while. I think he's just fishing a lot."

"He always loved fishing."

"You still fish?" he asks.

"Me? Have you seen this place? Besides, I only did it because you liked it so much."

"Well, I only did it because my dad liked it so much. You didn't enjoy it at all?"

I'm feeling warm all over and it's taking over, my mouth opening and it feels good open and saying, "I enjoyed what we did after..."

He's smiling a weird stone-smile that has no heat in it—just a mask covering his embarrassment. What business do I have reminiscing about shit like that anyway? It was years ago. We're both different people now, aren't we? But the stone chips away, and he laughs, "I did too. We've had some times, you know…"

We're both smiling now. I don't know what is

going on. It's the diner all over again with my heart pounding and his hand in mine. I feel it. It's coarse and rough from the auto shop, but it's also warm. I look into his eyes and they're warm too.

"Medium jalapeno, right?" the waitress says, placing a pizza freckled with green slices of jalapenos in the center of our table.

"No, pepperoni," Jim says. "We ordered a medium pepperoni."

"Just wait a minute," the waitress replies, digging into her apron and retrieving her notepad. She squints at it, and then squints at Jim. "No, no, this clearly says one medium jalapeno pizza with extra jalapenos."

"Extra jalapenos?" he scoffs. "We didn't want any!"

"Why did I bring this out then?"

"I don't know. That's between you and the cook back there." He's getting flustered, but he's trying to keep it in check. His mouth always goes super stiff when he gets frustrated—like some kind of exaggerated frown.

I turn to the waitress. "It's fine. We'll take it."

The waitress nods and walks away.

Jim looks at me, his mouth open and tilting upward in a sly, knowing way—in an old way. "She likes the spicy does she?"

"I just don't want to sit here and watch you argue over a pizza."

"I was about to have her bring us the right one. I just had to wear her down a little more..."

"Please. You're wearing me down. Are you

hungry or what? This place got good reviews or something, right?"

He raises his eyebrows, brown and full, but thinner too. "That's what it says." He picks up a slice and takes a bite. Several of the bright green circles go with it. He blinks his eyes several times, swallows, and takes a huge swig of water. He swallows again, and I think the worst of it must be over, but he brings the glass back up to his mouth and drains it.

"Are you okay?" I laugh.

"It's hot," he says, nodding his head, panting. "Really, burning hot. Like a fire in my mouth."

I can't bring myself to leave. It's 11:00 at night and I'm sitting on the small couch in Jim's hotel room. I want a hit so bad but I've resisted so far. I didn't even bring it with me so there's no use anyway. It's back in the nightstand—back with the Silver-Sin Eater.

He's in the bathroom. The door's closed and the light's flooding into the dark from the crack underneath the door. I can hear him faintly pissing. How did it come to this? Him being here and me sitting in his hotel room far past dark. Us picking up and talking like before—talking about books and movies and funny stories from the tall grass and the house and the pond and fishing. Talking just like before but with years between us. But that distance of years seems more and more insignificant with each passing second...

He comes out of the bathroom wearing a white t-shirt and boxers. Are we this comfortable with each other? He's walking around casually enough, scratching his chest as he bends down to the mini-fridge.

"Thirsty?" he asks, bringing out a tiny bottle of Scotch.

"Sure," I say.

He brings out a second bottle, hands it to me, and sits next to me on the couch. He holds it up, the cap open and fuming. "Cheers."

I take the cap off of mine and we both drain them in one gulp. He gets up and goes back to the fridge. "There's more where that came from."

"You know those things are super over-priced, right?" I say.

He hands me another. "It's a celebration. How often do I get to see you?"

We drink almost the whole fridge—not enough to get wasted, but enough to feel it. It's hitting me harder than usual—maybe because of the stress of everything. I'm not sure. I'm still in control though. My eyes feel heavy, and my head finds its way to his shoulder and rests on the bony part. I move, but I can't get comfortable. He slumps down and I follow, resting it instead on his chest.

"How are you?" he asks in a whisper.

I look up into his face, framed by the brown of his hair kissing the top of his eyebrows. "Just fine," I say, helpless against the smile I can feel breaking through from the sides of my cheeks.

"I'm glad."

He's warm and strong and I can feel myself slipping into sleep. I let it come, and, for a brief moment before, there is no Phil and no black-suited men and no dead bodies in penthouse apartments. There is no fire, and no cloud. There's just the warmth and the promise of a pleasant dream.

I'm wet. It's been raining and I don't have an umbrella. I left it at the apartment, which is just about the only place I can think about right now—getting home, making myself a cup of tea, and sitting down in front of my computer to write. It's all I want. No more of this dripping, sopping cold. The subway isn't appealing to me—too many other wet bodies all huddled up together giving each other pneumonia and turning the train into a greenhouse. I hold up my hand as a taxi drives by.

It stops—the red of its brake lights refracted by the water—and I walk.

"How ya doing, luv?" the driver says as I climb into the car. He has an English accent, which is surprising. I haven't heard one in person before.

"Fine, thanks," I answer. "Can you take me to Tatar Heights?" No, it's not Tatar Heights. What is Tatar Heights? I look down at my wet shoes. I can't remember where I live.

"That nice place downtown? Sure thing," he says, slamming the car into gear and speeding off—the engine thumping beneath us like an enormous metallic heart.

As we drive, I can start to smell it. It's faint at first, but it's growing stronger by the second. It looks like a trick of the eye—a wafting discoloration that spirals around the backseat and center console. Then the smell gets stronger and there's no denying it. Smoke. The car is filling with it, spewing out of the air vents and getting recycled again and again, each time a little darker, a little blacker.

"Can we open a window?" I ask.

"What's that?"

"Can we open a window?"

He smiles in the rearview mirror and it's Phil. I'm shut silent. "You want to air out?" he says.

I don't answer. My eyes are watching his. They're fluctuating in color. Flashing black and brown. I can't tell if it's me. I watch more.

"You want to air out?" he asks again, and pulls the car off to the side of the road. I hadn't noticed where he was taking me—I was too busy watching the mirror—but now we're here. It looks like an abandoned industrial park, rows upon rows of large cream-colored buildings like huge aircraft hangars. We're parked between two near the back. Their walls block out the sun.

The locks on both sides of the car engage, and the man turns back to me. I can see his face—old and gray. He puts his leather hat over the passenger seat and descends upon me. He slides over and inside my body but I'm not in it. I'm gone. Vacant. I'm just an empty shell, my eyes unseeing but fixated on a photograph pinned to the sun visor above the driver's seat. It's him, the man with the leather hat, the taxi driver, but he's younger and standing with two women—his arm around both.

Their hair is up in beehives and their eyes dark with makeup. I think about them—their lives. I wonder what they did after the photo was taken. I wonder how they met the man, and I wonder what they would say if they knew what he was doing to me. I've only been in the city a week.

I shoot awake as something rough brushes against my ankle. My pants are down. They fall off with a rustle on the carpet of Jim's hotel room. I'm in Jim's hotel room, I remember. His face is inches from mine, inching closer—his lips aiming for mine.

"No," I whisper.

"No?" Jim asks.

"No." I get up and grab my shoes by the door.

"Why not?"

"I just can't. Not now."

"It's been such a long time..."

"I know." I open the door.

"Where are you going?"

I walk out and close the door, his question echoing violently in my brain.

By the time I get to the street it's 1:30 at night, so I know they'll still be raging. I need a rager. The elevator of the building is broken again like it always is so I take the stairs all the way up to the 14th floor. I'm panting, drenched in sweat by the time I get to Room 149. I don't think there's any A/C. Maybe just the window mounted units people bring out during summer. But there's no windows for mounting in the stairwell—just a fluorescent light that flashes off and on every few seconds.

The music is blaring—some low-tempo hip-hop beat—I can hear it through the wood. I knock on the door and a pimply faced twenty-something in a white t-shirt and jeans answers. Saying nothing, he steps aside and I walk in.

Everyone is here—all the nameless faces I recognize from around town. There's the tall brunette with a different boyfriend. There's the Nazi-looking man always out of his mind. There's the two blondes who always become lesbians after a hit or two—mostly for the crowd—and there's a hundred thousand others, all huddled and throbbing with their eyes rolled back in their heads and fire in their veins and snow falling from their nostrils. I'm one of them, at least for tonight.

"Haven't seen you around for a while," Jakey says. I'm not sure what his real name is. Jakey is the name he uses when he's selling. He's the reason I'm here. His eyes are like tiny slits swirling in ether.

"You don't happen to have anything for me, do you?"

"That depends on what you have for me," he says, wobbling slightly.

I look around at the gyrating bodies, the two of us standing motionless in the sea. "This is a party, right?"

He scoffs and smiles. "Twenty-four hours a day. Seven days a fucking week."

He digs into his pocket and pulls out a bag of

white powder, saying, "I got you, baby bird." He sets a line up to his hand and brings it to my face.

I breathe in deep. "Shit, man..."

"Good shit, right?"

"Shit..."

"The next one ain't charity." He turns around and blends into the crowd and I'm left alone buzzing my head off.

I feel good for the first time in a while—a long while. The thumping music and the people let me forget and I sit down on the floor against the wall and just feel good. There's no taxi driver with the picture and the hands over me, and there's no Jim bringing it all up again—everything—and making me jittery and confused. There's just me. I feel damn good.

"You got a cigarette?" someone asks me. He's standing over me, but I don't look up. I can barely make out the words. The room is so loud and he's talking so quiet.

"No," I answer.

"You want one? You look like you want one."

"Sure, if you're offering."

"I am."

I stand up, my face inches from his. My whole body shakes and my throat runs dry. He takes out a cigarette and rests it on the end of my lower lip, lighting it with a match. "How have the last couple of days been treating you?" Phil asks.

My mind goes blank. "Uh, good, I guess. Well, as good as I can hope, all things considering."

"That makes me happy," he says, taking a long

drag of his own cigarette. He ashes onto the floor.

"I'm glad to see you got out alright," I say.

"Oh, I got out alright." His teeth are clenched. "I always fucking get out alright, alright?"

"Alright."

"I'm surprised you did, though." He relaxes. "Last I saw you were running—running faster than I thought a skinny thing like you could."

"I guess I got lucky."

"I guess."

I want to run again, faster than before and never stop until I know I'm safe—until I'm somewhere I know he can't find me. Wherever that might be. Chuck was right. Phil is going to kill me. I can see it in everything. In the way his lips tighten around his cigarette, and the way he squeezes his left hand with his right between drags. It's in it all. All in all.

He checks his watch and smiles. "Damn. It's still early. You don't have anywhere you've got to be anymore, right? Not since you quit your job at the department store?"

Has he been watching me? He must be. How else would he know? I don't say anything. I just smile, hoping he doesn't see the frantic energy beneath.

"I'm sure Mr. Neaves must be missing his star employee, huh?"

I laugh, but it's too short. "I think he'll manage to get by."

"Why'd you quit anyway? That was right after Chuck called you, right? How's he doing? I heard he got picked up."

"I haven't talked with him."

"You haven't talked with him?"

"No."

"That's not what he told me."

"What'd he tell you?"

"He told me everything. Said he met up with you outside of town. Said he told you to stay away from me."

I don't answer. There's no chance of a smile now. My face is flushed and white. He has to know. He has to know what happens next.

"I'm right, aren't I? It was difficult to make out through his screams, but I'm right. Aren't I?"

I only breathe.

He grabs me by the back of the head and shoves my face into his. "AREN'T I?"

I can't hold it in any longer and I burst into tears. "Yes. Yes, you're right. You're right. Just please don't hurt—"

"I'm right, aren't I?" he screams, shaking me. The music is blaring. "He told you everything. Told you of our little trip down to Havana, right? Told you the whole story."

Maybe there's hope. I cling to it with all that I have, the words flying out of my mouth fast and shrill. "What? No, no. He didn't tell me any of that. I don't even know what that is. I—"

"Shut up," he says, his grip tightening. "Shut up and quit lying to me. I know when you lie and when you tell the truth."

"I'm telling the truth now. He just said that you

put something in his food and that you're coming after him and that I should stay away from you. That's all he said, Phil, I promise that's all he fucking said."

"That's all he fucking said?"

"That's all."

He lets go of my head and I slink back towards the wall. He mutters something to himself, smiles, and lights up another cigarette. He breathes in long. "You want to go for a ride? The city's lovely at night."

"No. No, please. Phil, I—"

"I think you need some fresh air. It'll help you calm down. Help you think straight."

The room is swirling—spinning out of control. Everyone's crashing into everyone else. "Please, Phil. Plea—"

He reaches into the back of his pants and brings out a gun, pressing it hard against my temple. It's freezing cold. "I'm not asking, you know."

My eyes scan the room wildly, looking for someone—anyone—that sees what is happening. The music is blaring and they're all too fucked up. No one sees anything. No one sees more than a few inches in front of their damn face. Or maybe it's not registering. How is it not registering? How is no one seeing?

"To the door," Phil says, thrusting the gun into my back.

My feet move without me, carrying me out of the apartment. The hallway is dim as we make our way down the stairs. Our feet clang, making echoes that bounce along the narrow passage and reverberate—loud and strident—in my ears. Is Chuck dead, then? Phil had heard him screaming. He definitely alluded to Chuck being dead. Did he get to him? Why? I thought they were friends. Why is this happening? Why, for the love of God, is this happening?

We get to the bottom of the stairs and Phil pushes me to the door leading out to the street. I hope beyond hope that there's a cop out there, or someone that can help—someone who's aware of their surroundings and knows a look of distress when they see one. There has to be someone like that out there, and I have to have that look on my face. It has to tell them.

As the door swings open, I realize that there is no one—just a passed out homeless man leaned up against the wall. We go right along the sidewalk and, as we walk by him, I whisper, "Help me." I think he heard me. He's sitting up, looking around the street—first to the left, then to the right. He's looking for the origin of the voice he just heard in his dream. It's me, dammit. I need you. We're walking away and I'm looking as he stands to his feet, scratching his head. I reach my arm back, reaching for him, but Phil snatches it away and turns my head and the man is gone. I manage to get a glimpse. He's sitting back down, tipping his hat back over his eyes. He'll slip back into sleep now, and maybe his dream will be about me. Some girl looking for his help. I'll probably take the form of someone from his past—his mind will make sense of it, but it won't be the right sense. It won't really be me.

Just a shadow.

We walk down an alley way. It dead ends. This is where he'll do it. It has to be. No one else is around. He spins me around and I'm facing him. "Tell me the truth," he says, his eyes wild and fire. "What did he tell you?"

"I told you what he tol—"

Suddenly, bursting with noise in the dark, there's the sound of a bird. A mourning dove. Its coos echo down the alleyway.

Phil spins around, eyeing the corners of the buildings wildly. "No, no, no," he says. "They aren't supposed to be here—not yet. I'm supposed to be clear."

The sound increases in volume, but, strangely, I can't tell where it's coming from. It sounds close— so close that I should be able to hear the flapping of the bird's wings. I don't. There's just the singular call, but growing louder—louder without form or shape.

"You're not supposed to be here!" Phil shouts, and then begins firing—firing his gun at the corners of the buildings, filling the night with sound and light. He keeps shooting until there aren't bullets left. He's haggard, sweating, panting. He spins around and around wildly, his eyes always on the corners. "I fucking see you, fuckers!" he shouts. "I see you!"

I've had enough. As he reaches down into his pocket for something I take off. I run past him and turn left out of the alley, back the way we came. I can hear his feet fly after me, echoing out of the alley, united with desperation. "No, no, NO!" he shouts. "This isn't happening!"

I don't look back. I keep moving—past Jakey's apartment, the music thumping faintly through the brownstone.

"Get back here!" I hear echoing behind me, interspersed by the sound of the occasional car engine.

I don't go down into the subway. I don't want to risk being trapped at the platform. Instead, I keep running—my legs aching and burning. I go uptown. I don't think he's behind me anymore—at least, I don't hear him. That's not enough for me, though. I keep going, not looking back and not thinking of anything but getting to that hotel lobby. Jim's hotel lobby.

I see it up ahead—the light streaming out like some kind of beacon in a sea of night. I go straight past the clerk and make my way to the stairs. I'm not bothering with the elevator.

When I get to his floor, I slam into the door leading inside and run to room 347. I had memorized it. I don't know why, but that's not true. I know exactly why. I pound on the wood.

"Jim, Jim, it's me! You need to let me in right now!"

Is it just my imagination? It has to be. It can't be real. I hear footsteps coming up the stairwell. The metallic ring. They're moving fast.

"Ji—" I don't even get the word out. The door

is open and I throw myself inside. I throw myself into his arms.

"Marie, are you—"

"Close it. Close the door," I say, waving wildly.

He closes it, and I engage both of the locks. I think I'm safe now. I'm in his arms again and he's looking down at me with those big brown eyes and squeezing me more and more into him. I relent. I don't retreat. I accept it. Closer and closer we grow until his neck angles his head down and his hand lifts my chin to his lips.

We collide over and over and over, our bodies pale and glistening in the dark.

We lie together, naked and cocooned in the sheets of the bed. The sun came up hours ago, and my eyes are open and staring at the ceiling as it grows lighter. Jim's still asleep, snoring lightly.

I know I should tell him. I need to tell someone. I can't do it alone. I can't. I'll be dead soon. I open my mouth. "Someone is after me," I say.

He turns in his sleep, grunting. The moment's gone.

I climb out of bed and get dressed. My clothes reek of sweat and the sticky summer. Maybe it's for the best that he's not awake. I'll slip away, and it will be like he never happened—again. It'll be like he never happened again.

I slip on my shoes and head to the door. He

makes a noise—not a loud noise—just a slight wheezing sound. I wait. I don't know why I wait, but I wait for another sound. After that one comes another, and I stand by the door, my hand on the handle, waiting for more. I'm helpless until they come. Finally, one has words.

"Marie, you still here?"

My voice croaks, "Yes."

"Come back."

I walk to the side of the bed and stop. He sits up, shifting his weight to his side. I sit down next to him and he wraps his arm around me. "Were you leaving just now?" he asks.

"No. Of course not."

"Look at me." He grabs me by the back of the head and turns me towards him. "I know you. Tell me what's wrong."

He doesn't know me. He doesn't know me at all. Maybe he did—once—a long time ago. But that's only a maybe and he sure as hell doesn't know me now. I don't know why he thinks he does. People change. I sure as hell have, and I'm sure he has too...somewhere.

"I told you already, but you were sleeping."

He laughs. "Well, that doesn't count. Tell me now when I'm listening."

"Someone is after me. They tried to kill me last night. They almost did."

"You mean, when you left?"

"Yes."

"It was late."

"Yes."

"You shouldn't have gone out alone."

"I go out alone all the time. I live here. I've lived here for years. I'm not an idiot. I know where the bad places are."

"Still, you—"

"This wasn't a fucking mugging, Jim." The tears are coming. I'm trying to hold them back, but I'm not doing a good job. "Someone is trying to kill me. Stalking me."

He sighs, his eyes downcast—fixed on a dark stain on the carpet. "Who would want to hurt you? Are you in some kind of trouble?" His words grow darker. "Is it like Samantha said?"

Fucking Sam. "What did Samantha say?"

"Nothing."

I hold his face in my hands. I make him look at me. "What did she say, Jim?"

He leans in close to kiss me. "You're so bea—"

"No, Jim." I push him away, but I've still got him. I still have him by the face, my nails grazing his temples. "Tell me."

"She said that you're a-a prostitute. That you're whoring yourself out to some older guy."

I let him go, and he reels backwards. "No. That's not true," I say. "Never was."

Sam's back in my apartment. Not Chuck's—mine. The one I was able to afford for all of four months when I first moved to the city. The other eight were earned in less than pleasant ways. Bill Byer wasn't the worst of it.

He's over and I'm blowing him in the bedroom. I hear a knock on the front door and it's Sam. I hope that it's not—that it's some package being delivered or something—but I know it is and my knowing is confirmed when I hear her perky voice call out to me, "Marie, you in there? It's me."

There's no time and I have to finish or I don't get my money so I kick it in to overdrive and hope he doesn't think I'm rushing. He doesn't seem to notice and comes just fine, making that weird pained face that's his signature—that I've come to know so well.

"You're a family friend—just visiting for the afternoon," I tell him as we make our way to the door. He looks confused, but he nods as he wipes the sweat off his forehead and catches his breathe.

He's fumbling with his wallet now. Fuck. I don't need this. She's pounding and she's heard us. She heard us walking up.

"Marie, are you in there?" she says.

I open the door just as he slips me two twenty-dollar bills. He's always generous.

She walks in and, for only a brief moment, her eyes fall to the exchange—to the filthy semen-stained scraps of green that mean so much to me nowadays. I never cared about the shit before. But it's come to mean so much. More than anything else.

"This is Bill," I tell her. "He's a family friend. He was in the city so he stopped by for a little. He's got to get going now, though."

Bill nods and waves awkwardly as he walks out the door. I slam it like a tomb behind him.

She doesn't drop it—not in her head. She's

thinking about it all through the evening into the night. It's spinning wheels around and around in her head, churning and fermenting until it's ready—until 11:00 at night when we're walking to another club and we've already spent plenty of filthy green scraps that I don't have any business spending—not with my pantry empty and rent far past due. But I have appearances. I've never been hungry. I'm not a hungry person. I've never been poor. I'm not a poor person.

"Why did that man give you money?" she asks, and then the dam bursts. The water comes crashing down—thousands of gallons—rushing, rising. It runs through the tall grass and washes that Dutch Colonial house away—smashing it into a thousand tiny pieces on the rocks. Sam leaves. She gets a bus and gets the fuck out. Says she doesn't know me anymore. She doesn't realize that I don't know me either.

"Never was," I say again to Jim—Jim who's making the same face as Sam did before she left. The last face I ever saw her make.

He smiles and brings me in close. His voice is choked, whispering, "I'm so glad."

———————

I remember asking Chuck once while we were lying in bed. "I'm not supposed to trust them, right?"

"Nah, you can for most of them, actually," he said, wrapping the belt around his arm. "They're usually too stupid to catch onto anything. You just have to be smart about it. If you need help, I mean. Otherwise, just deal with shit yourself."

The memory fades and we're standing outside the steps of the police station—a huge gray building with moldy Ionian-style columns. "We'll just go in and tell them what you told me," Jim says.

He holds my hand as he leads me up the steps. I guess that's a thing we do now. I'm all nerves. Tatar Heights. If they run my name, it'll come up maybe. Is that how it works? But I haven't been stopped yet. Maybe they don't know. His grip tightens as we arrive at the door. He pushes it open and leads me to the front desk. A female officer is sitting there, spinning a pencil in her hand. Other than the three of us, there doesn't seem to be anyone around.

"You need help?" she asks me, still staring at her pencil. Her eyes don't move.

Jim talks before I can. "Yes, we have reason to believe that someone—"

"Someone is trying to kill me," I say.

The officer looks up. "How do you know that?"

How else am I supposed to know? I lean against the desk. "Because he tried to kill me."

"Tried?"

"Yes."

"Tried how?"

"He had a gun."

"And he missed?"

"No. He walked me out of a party."

Jim looks at me.

"Boyfriend of yours?" the officer asks.

"Who?"

"The man walking you out of the party."

"No. No, not at all."

"Not even once?"

"No."

"Is he cute?"

I stare at the woman, looking for some break in her stone veneer. There isn't one. She's staring right back at me—expressionless. There's no sign that this isn't real—that she's playing some kind of sick joke on me. I try to keep my cool, but fuck it. "Is that pertinent? Really?" I say.

The officer scoffs. "I'm just trying to get a description, ma'am," she says. "I thought I'd speak to you woman to woman. You're not a lesbian, are you?"

I'm too confused to think up a better answer, so I just mutter, "No."

"Then please answer my question. Is he cute?"

"Kind of, I guess."

"Kind of how?"

"How?"

"Describe him to me."

"I don't know." I'm talking, but I don't know what I'm saying. The words are streaming out brainlessly to match the brainless nature of this conversation. "He's tall with black hair, I gue—"

"He got a big dick?" she asks, and she looks at Jim now. She's not just looking. She's staring. I watch as he shrinks into himself, turning his eyes away.

"What? How would I know that?" I shout. I'm furious.

"I told you, we never fucked or anything. He's not my boyfriend. He's trying to kill me!" I'm getting louder. I'm breaking from her. I don't have to take this shit anymore. She's not going to fucking help me anyway.

"There's no reason to raise your voice, ma'am," she says.

"Why are you asking me all this—all this shit, then?"

"For your information, ma'am," she says, emphasizing her vowels in a short, condescending way, "there's a killer with a really big dick who's been going around killing. He's pretty hot too. Here," she reaches into her desk and produces a photo—blown up to almost a whole sheet of paper, "take a look."

He is very attractive—tall, dark, handsome—but he's not Phil.

"I take it that's not your guy?" the officer says, putting the photo back into the drawer of her desk.

"No," I answer—quieter than before.

"Okay. So who's your guy?" She brings out a pad of paper and a pen.

Maybe we'll get somewhere now. "His name is Phil. At least, that's how I know him. I never got a last name."

Suddenly it's as if a shadow comes over her— creeping up from the floor and digging itself in, writhing and wriggling up to her face, leaving her eyes for last. She swallows, and then says something I don't catch. The sound is too whispered. Too rasping.

"What was that?" I ask.

She breathes in deep and says, "What name again?"

"Phil," I answer, slower than before. "I don't have his last name."

"No. There's no one like that."

"What do you mean?"

"We don't know any Phil," she says, rushed and tucking her pad and pen back into her desk. "We're not aware of any perpetrators by that name."

"Are you kidding me?" Jim chimes in. His brow is furrowed in that way it always is when he's mad. In that way it always was. "Phil? You don't know of anyone named Phil?"

"No, sir. Now please lower your voice."

He continues—he's on a roll now, "Since when is it your job to cross-reference our account with yours? You're supposed to take our report and go look for the guy."

"Please don't tell me how to do my job, sir. And please lower your voice."

"Maybe I wouldn't have to tell you how to do your job if you would just—"

"Please LOWER your VOICE!" she screams. Is her gun out of the holster and pointing at him—only inches from his face? It is, but then, just as soon as it is, it isn't anymore. It never was. It's still in the holster on her side. The strap is still over the handle, too. It never left.

"Ma'am, I'm sorry," Jim says. His face is white and he's stepping rapidly away.

"You can leave now," the officer says—quiet, solemn. "We've got your report. Don't worry. We're on the job."

"Do we get a copy or anything?" Jim asks.

"Leave, please," she answers him.

We leave, and Jim paces awkwardly in front of the glass doors that lead inside. He's muttering something to himself—something about "I never" and "this wouldn't happen back home." I'm not listening. I'm watching. I'm watching the officer as she looks around the empty room. She's looking as if her life depended on it—as if there were mines or tripwires jutting out of every corner and hiding underneath every lonely file on every lonely desk. I watch her eyes, too. There's fear in them—real and tangible. She's afraid of something.

I watch as she makes a telephone call, but I can't make out the words. It's a short one—no more than ten seconds. There're no hellos or goodbyes. Just her saying a single word and nodding her head over and over. Then she hangs up.

"You want to go back to the room?" Jim asks, breaking me from my stupor. "We could call out for some food."

"No," I say. "No, I don't want to go back there." Something about being alone with him doesn't sit well with me. I need people—lots—and wide open spaces. I need space to see Phil coming for me, and I need people to hide. I can only look out for me.

"Let's go walk by the pier," I say. "We can get a funnel cake or something."

— — — — — — — — —

I can only look out for me. The police won't help me. Jim certainly won't—can't. I'm alone. At least I have my Silver Sin-Eater, somehow. Some strange way. But that's back at the hotel room—my hotel room, the one with the pipe that might have been a bomb. It seems more and more likely, but it also seems more and more likely that I'm losing myself to this—all this shit. For as much as he was a fucking idiot, Dr. Braxton was right. I'm not well, I think.

We're walking along the pier. I writhe my hand away and he doesn't bring his back. He puts it in his pocket, and walks with his face downcast for the most part. Silent.

We move past families and small children who run to the food stalls and attractions that pepper the pier. Their shouts and squeals help sober me a little. They're grounding in a way I can't explain. Maybe it's simply because there are people that are happy—carefree. I haven't been that way in a long time. I was once. At least, I'm pretty sure I was.

"We passed one," Jim says.

"What?"

"You wanted a funnel cake, right? Wait here."

I watch as he walks over to a stall manned by a short stocky man with a mustache. I can't help but think that I could probably do a quick line—just duck behind one of the tents or something. It would only take a second. But I don't. I watch as Jim hands the man some money and receives a steaming pile of fried and powdered dough. He's smiling as he brings it over.

"Looks good, right?"

I nod. His smile. I'm catching it again. It's making me feel better. It does look good.

"Want to find a place to sit down?"

We walk along the far pier and sit down on a bench facing the water—out to sea. It's a giant lake, the past grown to absurd proportions just like the two of us. He puts his arm around me and then his head bends down and his lips kiss my neck.

"Jim," I say.

"What is it?"

"I don't know. I just don't." I can't help it. I start to cry. He holds me closer and I let him. Birds sing out high overhead, but I can't see them.

"Do you remember that night we took your dad's truck out to Mt. Bear?" he says quietly, in a voice as smooth as silk.

"Yeah."

"And you wanted to drive up that trail so bad..."

"There were stars there."

"Mhm. There was that bald patch in the woods. Most of it was so thick and overgrown that you couldn't see a thing. It was so dark. But there was that one empty patch in the tree line."

"They were so bright, and that path looked like it was leading right up to them."

He holds me tighter. "Just that tiny dirt path," he says. "Barely there."

"I wanted to drive up there to them."

"You were also high as hell."

"Well, yeah..."

"And got the truck stuck."

"Yeah, but—"

"Your dad was pretty mad."

"He got over it," I laugh. "I'm still shocked he didn't find out about the drinking."

"I'm not so sure he didn't," Jim says. "He gave me this weird look when we were behind the truck trying to push it out. At one point I asked 'Are we pushing?' and I think a big hot whiff of beer shot out of my mouth. He must have smelled it. He didn't say a word to me for a few weeks after that."

"Shit, you're right! You were all worried that he wasn't going to let you in the house anymore."

"He still did though."

"I would have let you in anyway. There's nothing he could have done about it."

"I know you would have," Jim says, and then our lips connect for a long time and for a long time I'm happy. I'm happy because I'm not thinking. I'm just feeling his warmth and his moist lips slide along mine.

"You don't need to worry," he says.

"I know."

The funnel cake grows cold as we sit and watch a little black-haired girl bounce a big red ball on the wood of the pier.

We go back to his hotel room and he takes off my clothes and lays me down on the bed. He goes down on me and he's good but I can't focus. I can't enjoy it because of the swirling thoughts that fly around my head, bombarding me endlessly.

"Why are you here?" I ask him. He's just pulled up to the house in his car, and he's wearing his old white t-shirt, stained with oil from working in the garage. I run out to him and Digger runs out too, barking after him but it's not the past any more. This is now. And it has been twelve long years.

"Down here?" Jim laughs.

"No," I say, grabbing him by the ears and bringing him up to me. "Why are you here—in the city?"

He smiles and kisses my neck. "Because I love you," he says.

"No, I don't think so," I say. I let him go.

He crawls back to me. His hand rests on my thigh. "Are you alright?" he asks.

"Yes."

"I do love you, Marie. I mean it," he says, speaking soft and slow. "I'm sorry if we're moving too fast. I just feel like we never left. Remember all the times we had? It seems like they all happened last week. They're so vivid. I've been looking for you for a long time." He pauses and breathes. "I mean, of course I gave you space when you first moved out here with everything that happened, but I never stopped. I never stopped loving you."

It's not possible is it? The dark cloud, smoking, burning. Was Jim waiting just beyond it all this time? Waiting for me? If I had just checked...Maybe it would be over now. Maybe we'd be happy together. Maybe we could be. Maybe we still can.

"You mean that?" I say, the words coming out heavy and hard.

"Yes," he answers. "I do."

We make love and I guess that's what it—what it's always been. When we're finished he stumbles into the bathroom to wipe off and I sit. Maybe I should give him a chance. I'm beginning to feel like I used to, I think—tinged only by the passing of time. It leaves the whole thing with a strange aftertaste—like a diet soda or something. I can tell it's what I remember, but it's changed. I guess I just have to get used to it.

His cellphone rings from the pocket of his discarded pants on the floor. Naked, he storms out of the bathroom and grabs it. "I'm expecting a call," he says, throwing on his pants. He struggles with one of the legs.

"Hello," he says, answering the phone. He's still struggling as he wobbles to the door. "No, no. Hang on for one minute, alright? Alright. I hear you."

He sounds defensive—on edge. He finally gets the pants on and slips shirtless out the door. I can hear him—yelling. He's screaming almost at the top of his lungs, but he's walking further away so I can't make out the words. I sit and listen. It's only faint murmurs.

He cut his finger working on a car with his dad. Not his finger, his thumb. He cut it on some sharp part of the mail truck's undercarriage and he hasn't even cleaned it—just wrapped it up in toilet paper and duct tape. The paper's flaking off in dark crimson, and the tape flaps uselessly in the air.

"You didn't have a bandage?" I ask.

"I was trying to keep it tight."

I go into the bathroom and get some alcohol and a box of bandages. When I get back he's sitting on the bed, holding my eighth grade graduation picture in his hand—his bloody hand. He's getting little bloody fingerprints on the frame.

He smiles, "Hey, remember..."

After a couple of minutes I hear his voice getting nearer. He has the key. The electronic lock buzzes and he walks in.

"I'll see you soon," he says, and hangs up the phone.

"Who was that?" I ask.

"Some idiot from the garage. He needed help with something."

"You were yelling pretty loud."

He leans in close, and kisses me on the nose. "I'm supposed to be on vacation."

We get dressed—me still in the same clothes. I haven't stopped by the apartment to change. I can't. Even if the cops aren't onto me, Phil is. He proved that, and he knows where I live. That place is dead to me now. It has to be. Jim knows that. Plus I think he likes to keep me close. He's gotten possessive, but it's not Chuck's possessive. It's different. It's warmer, and I think it comes from a good place.

He takes me to Bastion's to get some new clothes, and he gives me his credit card. Trusts me with it. I don't think there's a single person I'd trust with a credit card, at least not in this city. But, then again, he's not from the city. I don't want to do him wrong, so I get a pack of panties and stick to the sale racks for the rest. I don't know what his limit is or how well he's doing financially. From what I remember, the garage was never that profitable. Mr. Bridges barely skated by.

It's awkward, but I change in one of the dressing rooms right after I check out—just walk right back into the interior of the store. The clerk looks at me strangely as I go into the stall, but I don't meet her eye. I just close the door fast behind me.

I change, and, despite being on the sales rack, it's much nicer than anything I've worn in years. Just a black dress—a slight neckline with exposed shoulders. The dress comes down to the middle of my knees and makes me look normal again. I look like the women on the street—not the ones running into tall banks or jewelry stores, but just the ones walking. Just normal. I do a line—a small one. It's all I have left.

Jim said he wants to take me out to dinner and I told him to pick a place. I hope it's better than pizza but I could go for anything right now. I'm as empty as a pill bottle.

He's waiting for me outside the store, standing

next to a gyro stand. "You look great," he says, and I smile because I feel great for the first time in a long while.

"Where do you want to go?" he asks.

"I thought that you were picking."

"Downtown?"

"You're picking."

"Downtown it is, then."

He raises his hand into the sky to call a taxi, but the black cloud is there. It swoops down from the stratosphere and takes it clean off. Bloodless and twitching, the hand falls to the ground while the cloud hovers above—just above Jim's head. He's standing motionless—unblinking—as a yellow taxi cab turns onto the avenue.

It's far away but idles closer—slowly. Its headlights burn like the sun. I don't need to see the driver to know who it is.

He drives by at a snail's pace, his leather hat fixed to his head and bobbing to the beat of some pop song playing faintly on the radio. He doesn't turn his head and look—he doesn't see me. He just idles on down the avenue, blissfully ignorant of me. The one he hurt.

"Let's take the subway," I say to Jim, viciously grabbing his arm and tugging it out of the dark cloud's body. His hand is back again.

"It's so hot though," he replies.

"It'll be cheaper."

"Please," he says, chiding. "You don't need to worry about that."

I take him by the hand and lead him

underground. The black cloud lingers on the street. I see it as we descend the stairs and it disappears from view. I know it follows us—follows us from the blighted sky. It knows all the train patterns, and it slides casually along as we're carried downtown in a train that is surprisingly empty for the time of day, casting a shadow of creeping smoke like a crosshair.

We ascend the stairs from the subway and it's gone invisible, but I still feel its presence.

"What are you feeling?" Jim asks.

"I told you. You're picking," I say. He grows silent and I'm worried I've offended him, but I don't have the capacity to tiptoe around his feelings right now. Seeing that man again—seeing him for real—it's shaken me like I knew it would. I've dreaded it. I've dreaded it ever since that day. In a city of over eight million people, I knew my chances were slim. But they were still there. They were still too high, apparently.

"Jim, can we just sit down for a minute," I say. I feel like I can't breathe. I need to catch my breath or I'm going to cry. Not just cry. I'm going to throw myself into the street. There's a truck coming, blasting Spanish music and honking. I'm going to do it. I can't take it anymore.

"Where are we supposed to sit down?" he says. He turns his head, his eyes landing on the homeless man on the corner, the light-pole, the stand with the man selling kabobs. His feet don't stop.

I sit down on the sidewalk—panting—my back against a newspaper rack.

"Hey, c'mon," Jim says, turning around and

offering me his hand. "You're going to get stepped on."

I bat it away, feeling vomit rising up my throat. I need air. "I need to lie down," I say. We're close to the Hotel Longhorn. I still have the key.

"Do you need to head back? We can head back."

"No, let's go over a few blocks. It's not far."

"What's not far?"

It's hard to form words so I stand up and motion for him to follow me. He takes me by the arm and we walk. When we get to the hotel I point to the lobby doors and he opens them for me. I'm feeling weak and achy. I know—I think—it's all psychological, but I still can't help the way I feel.

That fuck of a clerk is at the desk. "I thought you said there weren't going to be any guests," he says as we pass on our way to the elevators. He shouts after us as the doors close, "I'm adding the fee onto your bill!"

His words echo away as the elevator begins its slow ascent to the eighth floor. When the doors open, I lead Jim to the door with the white splotch instead of a number and I press the keycard against the reader. The door chimes open.

There was something in the corner—in the dark—before I switched the lights on. My finger was already in motion by the time I saw it, and it vanished immediately when the light hit it. It was crouching—hiding—its teeth bare and its fingers thin and long like shoelaces. They were grasping a gun and pointing it towards the door while Benjy

burned in his basinet at its side. Now both are gone.
I scream.

— — — — — — — —

There's movement, and I wake up. I must have
fallen asleep. Jim has the door open. Light is
streaming in from the eighth floor hallway.

"I have to go," he says.

There's someone else with him. A woman.

"I have to go," he says.

The woman just glares at me.

"Wait, you can't," I say. "I'm sorry. I don't
know what came over me. I just didn't feel well."

"Say goodbye, you fucking slut," the woman
says.

I look at Jim. I think he can see the surprise in
my eyes. He opens his mouth to speak to her but he
closes it again and lowers his head.

"You can ignore me all you want, but not when
I'm standing right in front of you, huh?" she says.

"I-I don't understand," I answer.

"It took me a little, but I knew where he was
going when he up and disappeared. And with me
being pregnant, too! He's been wanting to fuck you
for a long time. Calling you day and night. Oh, I've
been calling you too, but you never answer those!"

"I don't have a phone."

"You've got a goddamned number, that's for
damn sure!" She turns to Jim. "Let's go. You've
fucked around enough."

"I'm sorry, Marie," he says as he's pushed away.

She slams the door and her squealing voice is carried further and further away.

I climb out of bed—still wearing the black dress—and rush to the door. I open it, and see them waiting for the elevator to go down.

"Ji—" I begin, but I'm cut short by the look he gives me.

It's final. There is nothing in it but ends. It's the same look my father had—standing up at the pulpit with his head hung low. The long sigh. There is a spark there, dancing somewhere around his corneas, but it's dim and growing dimmer. It goes out altogether as the elevator chimes and the steel doors close around them.

A slight hum as the elevator slinks away. Then nothing but silence—a silence so thick it's oppressive. I feel like it's infecting me, making me silent. Even the beating of my heart makes no sound. The only sound I hear is the sliding of fingers along the floor—long shoe-lace fingers around a gun.

I go back into the room and get the Silver-Sin Eater. I put it in my purse underneath a pile of tissues.

I know where I'm going. I'm going where the fire burns hottest—that vestige of orange embers, hiding and burning underneath the ash. I'm going where that dark smoke-cloud was born—not born—but where it breeds.

When I get to the door I jiggle the key back and forth, trying to get it to stick. All the while I look around—my eyes wide like an animal's in high-beams. Phil's out there, breathing in the smoke that billows out from our open window. I think the window was left open. I can see it from the street. Chuck usually kept it open for when we smoked. I don't think it was ever closed.

Finally, it's in. Secure. I open the door and climb the stairs to our apartment in the dim light. I get to the door and, for some reason, I knock. Maybe out of some strange sense of humor. Not surprisingly, there's no answer.

I put the key into the lock and give it a sharp turn. The door opens and I walk inside. Directly in front of me—only a few feet from the door—is a tall metal stool. It's not my stool and it's not Chuck's. I've never seen it before. I hear a distinctive beep and a small black box that sits on top of the stool flashes red and then goes dead. I walk over to it and find that there are no buttons—nothing. Just the small red light slowly fading away. I can think of nothing but Phil's black keycard. I pull the Silver-Sin Eater out of my purse, but I won't be long. I can't be long.

Why now after all this time? I've known it was there—an enormous hand reaching out to me from the past—but I never took hold. I turned away because I knew its touch would burn. It would burn me alive—inside and out—and it would be like it was back then. But why now am I going over to the corner? Why now am I digging through the pile of dirty clothes? Is it because of Jim, or something else? Is it simply because it's time—fated—or am I just tired of running? Why now am I sliding the papers away? There are only a few of them. I printed them off right when I got to the city. They were hung up on the wall—inspiration—they still have the holes where the nails went through. Only twenty-three of them. There was going to be more. So many more. They were going to be imprinted on the minds of thousands and talked about in college classrooms. There would be billboards. I slide the pages away, my eyes falling on the top margin and the words that were meant to mean so much but smell like BO and semen-stained cotton,

HARD TIMES IN
A SMALL TOWN

I find it underneath. My cellphone, powering it up...

It's been plugged in the whole time—in case I needed it, I guess. The screen flashes blue and the notifications roll in. **58 unread messages**. Some are from before, but many are new. I open them and my eyes fly over the words as the heat slides underneath my skin. All mixed together as one all-consuming fire.

WHY ARE YOU IGNORING
ME, BITCH? COWARD!

WHERE ARE YOU?

I MISS YOU.

I KNOW ABOUT YOU TWO. DON'T THINK I DON'T.

HOPE YOU HAVE FUN WITH HIM ON HIS "BUSINESS TRIP." FUCK YOU!

MARIE, COME HOME.

DAD'S IN A BAD WAY. HE'S BEEN ASKING ABOUT YOU.

IT'S THE ANNIVERSARY, SWEETIE. TRY NOT TO BE TOO HARD ON YOURSELF. IT'S NOT YOUR FAULT. IT WAS A FREAK THING. PEOPLE SMOKE ALL THE TIME AND THEIR HOUSES DON'T BURN DOWN. IT WAS JUST BAD LUCK.

HAPPY BIRTHDAY! HOPE YOU'RE DOING ALRIGHT.

REMEMBER THAT TIME BY THE LAKE? ;)

HE HAS A WIFE!

DAD'S IN THE HOSPITAL
AGAIN.

ARE YOU COMING?

WHERE THE FUCK ARE
YOU?

WE LOVE YOU, SWEETIE.
ALWAYS.

I'M THINKING ABOUT MY
LITTLE ANGEL BENJY
TODAY...

HEY, I DON'T KNOW IF YOU'RE
IN TOWN BUT EVERYONE'S
GETTING TOGETHER FRIDAY.
LOVE TO SEE YOU THERE.

PRAY FOR YOUR BROTHER.
HE'S IN REHAB AGAIN.

I'M COMING TO THE CITY! YOU
STILL THERE? WE COULD
MEET UP! :)

I'VE BEEN THINKING ABOUT
YOU A LOT LATELY. DO YOU
STILL DYE YOUR HAIR WEIRD
COLORS? LOL

HOW'S THE WRITING GOING?
LET ME READ IT WHEN YOU
HAVE SOMETHING. I'LL GIVE
YOU AN HONEST REVIEW!

CHRIS GOT ARRESTED AGAIN.
WE DON'T KNOW IF THEY'RE
GOING TO LET HIM GET BAIL
THIS TIME.

PLEASE CALL ME.

HAPPY BIRTHDAY, SWEETIE!
YOU KNOW YOU ALWAYS
HAVE A HOME HERE.

MARIE, HE'S NOT DOING
WELL.

MAN, I LOVED THE TASTE OF
YOUR PUSSY.

WHO IS THIS?

DR. BRAXTON CALLED AND
WANTED TO KNOW HOW YOU
WERE DOING.

LET ME KNOW WHEN YOU'RE
IN TOWN NEXT. WE COULD

GET A DRINK OR SOMETHING!

THINKING OF YOU...IN ALL
THE NICE WAYS. ;)

SHIT, I'M REALLY FUCKED UP.
I THINK I MIGHT DO IT THIS
TIME. NOT THAT YOU GIVE A
FUCK. YOU NEVER ANSWER
ANY OF MY CALLS OR TEXTS
OR ANYTHING. JUST
DROPPED RIGHT OFF THE
FACE OF THE FUCKING
EARTH, HUH? YOU THINK YOU
CAN RUN AWAY FROM WHAT
YOU DID? I KNOW YOU DIDN'T
MEAN TO DO IT, BUT YOU'RE
KILLING US TOO, MARIE.
YOU'RE KILLING US BY JUST
PRETENDING THAT WE DON'T
EXIST.

WE LOVE YOU AND YOU'RE
SHITTING ON OUR FUCKING
FACES. YOU'RE NOT THE
ONLY PERSON WHO LOVED
HIM. WE ALL DID, AND WE ALL
LOVE YOU. FUCK. WHATEVER.
I THINK I'M DONE. WITH
EVERYTHING.

I KNOW IT WOULD MEAN A LOT
TO HER IF YOU'D COME.

MERRY CHRISTMAS, SWEETIE!

WHERE ARE YOU STAYING
THESE DAYS? I'M THINKING I
MIGHT COME UP.
I KNOW YOU PROBABLY
WON'T ANSWER, BUT I GUESS
THIS IS WORTH A TRY.

I SUPPOSE YOU HEARD. I'M
HOLDING UP ALRIGHT. WHAT
I'D LIKE MOST IS IF THE
WHOLE FAMILY COULD BE
TOGETHER. I KNOW YOU'RE
PROBABLY BUSY WITH YOUR
OWN LIFE, BUT I HOPE YOU
CAN MAKE THE TIME.

I'M SO ANGRY RIGHT NOW,
BUT I WANT TO MAKE IT
CLEAR TO YOU WHAT YOU'RE
DOING. WE'VE BEEN MARRIED
FOR 7 YEARS AND WE HAVE
THREE CHILDREN TOGETHER.
THESE LITTLE EXCHANGES
BETWEEN YOU TWO NEED TO
END NOW! I'VE TALKED WITH
HIM AND HE SAID HE'S NOT

GOING TO TALK TO YOU
AGAIN. I SUGGEST YOU DO
THE SAME.

WE USED TO FUCK LIKE
RABBITS.

WELP. DIDN'T WORK. I'M IN
THE HOSPITAL. BEEN IN A
COMA FOR A FEW DAYS.
FEELING ALRIGHT DESPITE
HAVING THEM STARING AT ME
24/7.

YOUR MOM'S WORRIED
ABOUT YOU. IT'D BE NICE IF
YOU COULD CALL US.

WE LOVE YOU, MARIE. I HOPE
YOU KNOW THAT. WHATEVER
YOU'RE GOING THROUGH.

HAPPY EASTER! HE IS RISEN!
MAY THE LORD SHINE DOWN
ON YOU THIS DAY AND EVERY
DAY! <3 <3 <3

JUST SAW THE CUTEST
HUSKY/LAB MIX. DID YOU
EVER GET ONE?

IT'S JUST ALL FUCKED.

DAD SAYS HE'S DOING
BETTER. HE SHOULD BE ABLE
TO LEAVE SOON.
I CAN'T BELIEVE YOU. YOU
DIDN'T EVEN SHOW UP. FOR
YOUR FUCKING DAD'S
FUNERAL. YOU PROBABLY
DIDN'T EVEN GET ANY OF OUR
CALLS OR MESSAGES AND YOU
PROBABLY WON'T GET THIS
ONE EITHER AND I DON'T GIVE
A FUCK IF YOU DO. I DON'T
KNOW WHY MOM KEEPS
ASKING ABOUT YOU (SHE
DOES KEEP ASKINGABOUT
YOU) BECAUSE YOU'RE A
FUCKING SELFISH BITCH AND
I HOPE YOU REALLY ARE A
FUCKING WHORE LIKE SAM
SAID.

ANY GOOD RESTAURANTS UP
THERE? I'LL TAKE YOU OUT
SOMEWHERE WHEN I COME
UP.

NOT LIKE YOU'RE GOING TO
ANSWER THIS. LOL.

THEY HAD A LOVELY
MEMORIAL SERVICE THIS
MORNING. WE JUST GOT
BACK. THERE WERE TWO
PICTURES. ONE OF YOUR
FATHER AND ONE OF HIM
HOLDING LITTLE BENJY. IT
WAS REALLY BEAUTIFUL. I
HOPE YOU CAN COME HOME
SOON.

OKAY. I'M THINKING MAYBE
NEXT WEEK? DOES THAT
WORK FOR YOU?

LOL. SORRY ABOUT THAT
LASR ONE. I MAAAAAAY HSCE
HAD A LITTLE TOO MYCH TO
DRN...LOL.
DAD DIED.

I THINK YOUR BROTHER IS
DOING BETTER. HE'S OUT OF
REHAB NOW AND HE'S EVEN
STARTED GARDENING! ISN'T
THAT FUNNY? HE HELPS OUT
AROUND THE HOUSE TOO! I
THINK THEY MIGHT HAVE
SENT ME THE WRONG BOY
BACK! JOKING, OF COURSE.
WE BOTH MISS YOU.

ARE YOU COMING TO THE
WEDDING? HAPPY BIRTHDAY!

WE LAID HIM DOWN RIGHT
NEXT TO BENJY. SHE WANTED
TO GET A FAMILY PLOT.
MOM'S NAME IS ALREADY ON
THE STONE. IT'S FUCKING
MORBID.

CAN YOU PLEASE PICK
UP!!!!!!!!!!!!!!!!

I KNOW YOU PROBABLY
WON'T GET THIS. I'M NOT
GOING TO MAKE IT. I JUST
WANTED TO TELL YOU
I LOVE YOU

I'm a whirlwind. A tornado spiraling out of
control, tearing the world apart. There has to be
some fucking shit around here somewhere. Chuck
always had a stash. Mostly just heroin and shit, but I
need a line. I'm running—running around the room
throwing clothes and discarded beer bottles and
pizza boxes and magazines and candy wrappers and
everything all around looking for a small plastic bag
I'm not sure even exists. I doubt it does. Haven't I
looked for it before—hundreds of times? The room
is spinning frantically all around me and I'm
absolutely losing it. I don't know if I'm standing still

or falling through the sky—a black sky with only a single cloud, a dark one billowing smoke and fire and sucking Benjy and now Dad up in it too. Dad...

I just needed something to show for my efforts. Something so that, when they came to visit, I could point to it and say "Look here, this is me. This is what I've been doing. This is the good that I've made for myself." But the more I lingered the more the cloud grew and the further and further I slipped...until this. Me running around the dilapidated, disgusting apartment of my dead boyfriend—looking for a corpse's blow.

I know I don't have much time. That black box is just staring at me from the stool. I want to smash it—throw it out the window and watch it splinter into a million pieces below—but I still don't know what it is. A bomb is all I can think of. I don't think its motion sensitive. My running would have already set it off. All I know for sure is that it reeks of Phil. He's been here, and he'll be back. He's probably on his way now.

Defeated, I slump down on the pile of clothes and the remains of whatever *Hard Times in a Small Town* had once been. Twenty-three pages of text— all tripe and meaningless. Mocking me. I rip them to shreds and, after I rip them, I rip them again. I take out Chuck's lighter from under the bed and burn them, the fire reminding me of the fire of before but I don't give a shit. I'll let it take me. Let Phil come. He can have me.

But I need to have my hit.

I stamp out the fire, grab my cellphone, and call

the only person in the fucking world who can help me now.

"Yeah," Bill Byer says.

"Hey, I'm in a bad way. Can you give me some money?"

"I gave you money."

"It's gone. I need more."

"I thought you needed a place to stay. I gave you that too." His voice is stone cold.

"I really need it. I'll do whatever you want."

"I want you to clean up and get sober."

"What?"

"This isn't like before, Marie. I'm finished with it all. The other night cemented it. I feel awful and I'm done. I'm out. I've got a kid now."

"You had a kid before."

"I mean another one. Look, I just can't anymore, alright?"

I say it softly. "Alright."

"I hope you get the help you need." He hangs up.

I throw the phone against the wall. It doesn't break. It just sits on the floor glowing blue and I guess it hit a button or something because it's playing its ringtone for some reason. It's a custom one. I set it before I left for the city. It's a little beeping and booping version of "Don't Worry Be Happy."

I light up a cigarette. Cigarettes. Strange that I still keep them so close. Of course I gave them up when it first happened. The smell actually made me sick to my stomach. But that changed. It changed shortly after I moved out here. Now I usually don't even think about them in relation to it. Usually. I sure as hell am now. I can't think of anything except coke and cigarettes and the fire and baby Benjy's crying but the flames are too high and too hot and for some reason they all wanted to go into his nursery. Maybe it was the stuffed animals all piled up in the one corner from the two birthdays he had—the only two he'd ever have. Then it was Dr. Braxton and the pills and losing my mind but getting it back I think and then moving out because mom was too sad to look at and I wanted to be a writer anyway and the city was the best place to do that because of all the publishing houses and all the different people just waiting to inspire me.

Now all of it, everything my life has culminated in, can be found in this tiny apartment. And it's not even mine. Fuck. I'm feeling the nerves again and the room is spinning and I feel like jumping out the window and splattering myself on the pavement—anything to make the feeling end.

Without warning, the black box on the stool beeps to red and the lock on the front door clicks open. I locked it. I know I locked it. I run to the bedroom as the door opens on its hinges. I peek through the crack of the bedroom door. I don't see anything at first—I only hear. Hear the soft creaking of steps on the floorboards. Hear the short, rasping breath. Then I see. Not all at first. Just a leg, then a hand. Then I see him: Phil—standing by the table where Chuck always did his crosswords. I can tell it's him, but he's all messed up and wrong. His eyes are bloodshot and his clothes are in tatters. His hair is balding or burned in some places and he looks emaciated—the bones of his face threatening to break through the skin. How he changed in such a short amount of time, I don't know. I don't know anything. There's nothing in me capable of knowing, of discerning—of putting two and two together. There's no room. I'm all filled with fear and apprehension and a sickening dread that tells me I'm going to die—that it's all over. That my time has come and whatever I've accomplished—the whole lot of nothing that I've made of myself—is about to be thrown to the wind, my body scattered and sucked down into the earth. Into the smoke and the cloud and the flames.

He closes the door behind him—slowly, softly—his eyes scanning the room, going from one side to the other, landing on each piece of furniture. He brings his arm backward and I hear the lock click shut. His mouth is that same twisted grin, but it's even more pronounced and looks disproportionate—like it's grown into his face. Slowly, he moves further in.

"I'm looking..." he whispers in a kind of sing-song way, crouching down low to the ground. "I'm looking."

There's something in his voice—in the way he moves—that unsettles me. He's like some kind of giant insect, his head pivoting on chitinous threads—twitching, writhing, searching. Searching for me.

I pull the Silver-Sin Eater out from my purse

and duck down along the side of the bed. I can't see him anymore, but I can hear him. He's tossing the table over, spilling its contents onto the floor. He's pounding near the kitchen sink and panting through clenched teeth, repeating in a sort of chant, "Looking...looking."

I tighten along the grip of the gun and suddenly the sounds stop. It's quiet—silence. I can hear the blood in my ears, and the sound of my breathing is like a wind tunnel. I swallow and it's like an explosion in my head.

Then, sobbing—faint at first, but growing louder. He's crying. I hear what sounds like his body slumping against the wall between the bedroom and living area, and he whimpers and cries on the floor. I can make out some of the words, but they come out raspy and full of air.

"You—know—didn't—can't—why—Chuck—kill—her—made—me—how—I—just—before—stuck—they'll kill me—cover it up—make it gone—come—sorry—so—sorry."

The sobs die down and I hear him slowly get to his feet. "Now," he sniffs. "Looking..."

I don't know what my options are, but he doesn't seem all there so I slowly inch towards the window that leads out to the fire escape. I don't know how long he'll be preoccupied with turning over furniture and sobbing on the floor, but if there's a chance I can get down to the street without him seeing me, I'm taking it.

I keep the gun pointed towards the door, and I can't help it. My hand shakes every time he makes a sound. He alternates between slamming and crashing and banging—and dead silence. It's the silence that I can't stand. Now I'm only a few feet away from the window. Then I have to open it and climb down without him knowing. That's the hard part but I have no other choice. There's no other way out. I reach, my fingers probing for the glass and the little switch that unlocks. I can't risk taking my eyes from the doorway. At last I find it and feel its coolness on the tip of my index finger. I look back to the latch to open and as soon as I do I hear his feet shuffling on the floor—shuffling frantically towards me. I turn and he's already there in the doorway, his gun pointed at me and his grin taking over nearly his entire face. How is that possible? It's growing, stretching—tearing the skin. I raise the Silver-Sin Eater but I'm not fast enough and the shot rings out, bringing with it thunder and fire and a burst of sharp pain that tears through my shoulder. I find the strength and I squeeze and fire shoots back from me this time, tearing into him somewhere but I can't tell where. I only know because his grin is gone and he's wincing in pain—wincing as he fires three more times, each accompanied by a burst of flame and sound and each tearing into me in new and terrible ways.

I cry out in pain, my back against the wall as the blood pours out—my voice raw and not my own. He walks—shambles, stumbles—over to me. I can see blood coating his shirt and running down his arm, dripping on the carpet. His eyes are glazed and his mouth is nothing but a tiny slit of lips and teeth.

The pain is too much. I'm sliding down the wall, my feet unable to carry my weight. His gun is in my face, and I look up into it—into the barrel. Into the dark. Soon there will be a fire inside that dark and then there will be nothing—nothing of me. I'll be gone.

He shakes, his mouth twitching wildly and his head bobbing up and down. "S-s-sorry," he says. He makes a gagging noise and his legs give out as he collapses onto himself into a combined pool of our bloods—mingling and churning together as both our lives are fading. Relief washes over me. I can breathe again, but the breath is shallow.

My eyes are growing dark—darker still. I can just make out the room and, to the left above my head, the window. My heart clings to it—is still clinging to it—despite everything. It's my only way out. The only way.

A wave of dizziness flies over me as I struggle to slide myself back up the wall. I can feel the holes—the raw shooting pain where the fire burned through—but I can't tell how bad they are. Large swaths of me are red and numb and tearing. The only feeling is weakness and pain and when one wave ends, the other begins.

I can't do it. My legs won't move. Maybe he got a nerve or something, or maybe I'm too weak. They're just sitting there, my dress soaking up the red. It'll have to be my arms, then. I reach around and try to grasp the lip of the window sill. My hands slip from all the blood, but I manage to turn myself around and latch onto the sill with both hands. I take a deep, shallow breath.

Mustering whatever strength I have left, I lift myself onto my knees, my tattered leg shooting pain up into the rest of me over and over.

My head is just high enough to look out. There's nothing—nothing but darkened windows and a few cars that zoom by below, their lights gliding apathetically over my building. But then—then...

I see a spark. It's faint, yellow—dancing slowly up...and then down. A spot of brightness in one of the black windows in the building across from me—a window on the second floor. I stare, and the light is all I see. It fills my entire field of vision and it reminds me of that night so long ago with the house in the tall grass and the fire and the smoke and my little brother burning and dying in it from a fucking cigarette. I look and see that there's also smoke around it—around the spark. There's the smoke and the fire and the spark is a cigarette too. It's the man across the way.

I breathe deep and push up on the window sill with my arms. It doesn't budge. It feels like all of me is breaking under the strain, and I know I'm losing blood fast. I know it because I'm growing lighter and the world is growing darker. Everything is growing darker except for the spark of cigarette light. I hope to God he can see me.

Raising my fists I pound on the glass with all my might. They slide off—the blood squeaking. It'll take more. It'll take the most I've ever given. It'll take all I have.

I raise my hands up high and send them colliding down on the pane of the window with full force. "Help me..." I scream, but the scream is so soft.

IV

I can't, for the life of me, remember what brand she likes. It's not a small distinction, at least to her. Buck-O or Luck-E is what I'm struggling with—both described in tiny letters as Crunchy Shredded Wheat Weaves Breakfast Cereal. I have to squint to read the words. I remember I brought the wrong one back one time and she took a bite and then just sat there at the table staring as it went soggy.

"This tastes weird, Ernie," she said.

"How does it taste weird?" I asked her. "It's what you like, right?"

She frowned in this over exaggerated way and shook her head like a little girl. I picked up the bowl and dumped it in the sink. I dumped the whole box out a few weeks later when it had gone stale.

So now the question is Buck-O or Luck-E? I put both in the cart. I bet they both taste like crap but I'll eat whichever one she doesn't like.

I grab a gallon of milk and a carton of eggs and head to the front of the store to the registers. When it gets to be my turn, I look up at the cashier in surprise.

"You're running this thing, Ed?" I laugh.

"Yeah. One of the girls called out. Left me damn near stranded." He smiles. He owns the place. He's a small man wearing a t-shirt and khakis and long dark hair on his arms. "You want your usual?"

I definitely do. "I shouldn't," I say.

"Of course you shouldn't, but you're still going to, aren't you?" He smiles, putting a pack of Marvin's into the bag with the eggs. "Judy still doesn't know?"

"I'm sure she knows, but she doesn't say anything. I don't do it in front of her. I wait until she's in bed."

Ed nods silently as he rings up the cereal and totals my order. "$35.68," he says.

I swipe my card. It seems like it keeps getting more and more expensive just to live, and I haven't gotten a raise from Saracen Construction in years. It doesn't help that each mayor increases the tobacco tax so they can look like they're on the side of "public health." Public health. What a load of crock. If they were really on the side of health they would take down those huge stacks that billow smoke or steam or whatever that stuff is out from the underground. I see them all the time—red and white striped poles like a barbershop jutting out of the asphalt. They stand maybe six feet high? I don't know what shoots out them. Sometimes it's gray like smoke, but other times it's white like steam. I read somewhere online that it could be chemicals the government's shooting in the air that calcifies the part of the brain that helps us commune with nature. I don't know about any of that. People get the strangest ideas...

Ed bags up the groceries and hands them to me over the counter. His arms wobble in the air and I notice how frail he's looking. "You feeling alright?" I ask.

"Of course," he replies. "Why wouldn't I be?"

I smile and leave the store.

Evidently, Ed's not the only one getting older. The three blocks back to our apartment nearly kill me. I can feel my heart heaving with each step, trying frantically to pump blood through arteries doubtlessly clogged by years of fast-food. It's usually the only thing in walking distance when I'm out on the job. The job. Also, where I first picked up smoking. Funny. I've worked all my life to have a life and it's exactly that working which will ultimately end it probably. That's some kind of paradox or something. I guess something has to end it eventually, though. Everything leads to an end of some sort.

The stairs are almost too much for me. Luckily there's only one flight.

"Which one did you get, Ernie?" Judy asks as soon as my head pokes through the door.

I walk inside and close it behind me before I answer. "I got them both. I couldn't remember what the one you liked was." I slip the cigarettes into the vase by the door before she can see.

"You never remember anything."

I put the cereal on top of the fridge and open the cabinet above the microwave.

"Can you get me a bowl?" she asks.

"I'm getting one." I take down one of the cheap plastic ones we've had forever. It's bright red. "You need to take your insulin first."

"It's in the bedroom."

"I know where it is."

I walk to the bedroom and grab her kit from the nightstand. Before every freaking meal. Crazy. I'd hate it if it were me. I think that every time, but, for her, she doesn't seem to mind. She's been diabetic for over thirty years, though. I doubt she remembers a before.

"You can do it for me?" she asks.

"Certainly, my dear," I say, bringing the kit to the table. I sit down across from her and take out one of the alcohol pads. She rolls the sleeve of her blouse up to the shoulder, her arm as firm and brown as it was forty-four years ago. I run the pad along and put the needle in. She looks at me and smiles. I always wince when I do it and she thinks it's cute.

I put the kit back on the nightstand and return to the kitchen. She's up at the counter pouring her cereal.

"You should sit back down," I say "I can get it."

"Let me move around while I can, Ernie. They haven't started yet."

No. Not till tomorrow. I sit down at the table. "Alright. What if I'm worried?"

"You're not the one getting it."

"But, for you..."

She walks over to my chair and I rest my head on her chest. She runs her hand along my scalp where the hair's become thin. "It'll be alright, Ernie-boy. People beat it all the time."

"And a lot of the time they don't."

She tilts my head up and kisses me. "We just have to hope. It's all we have."

As she walks back to her cereal I can see it already. Her bald head in a scarf—leaning over a trash can as she pukes up white liquid since there's nothing left in her stomach. After that it's tests, tests, and more tests and maybe some of them will help and then maybe some of them won't and then maybe some of them will help at first but then later we'll find out they didn't and it's spread—eating her alive, slowly.

And then maybe it'll go into recession. Not cured. Recession. Recession where we'll go back every few months and see if she's going to start dying all over again. I guess something has to end it eventually, though. I just want more time.

"Let's go to the beach," I say.

She looks up from her cereal. "The beach? You hate the beach."

"But you love it, right?"

"But you hate it!"

"But I love you."

She's staring at me, her mouth agape and her eyes puzzling. "You want to go to the beach?"

"Yeah. I want to go to the beach." The more I say it the more I want to. I want to see her in her bathing suit, smiling with sun bearing down on her body instead of death. She does love the beach.

"When?"

"Today. Right now."

She's still stunned. "Right now?"

"Right now. I can get Russ to cover for me. We can leave whenever you're ready."

"Is this because I have cancer?" she smiles.

I don't miss a beat. "Yep."

We're over the bridge and headed southeast. Judy is giddy like a little girl in the passenger seat and I think I'm catching it too. For a little while, I hope we can hold the future off. I think it will be easier for her than me. I'm having a hard time, but, as we leave the suburbs and the tightly-clustered rows of houses and buildings that steadily lose their levels, I feel a little better. I feel good that she's feeling good.

We drive over the dunes and get to the parking lot next to Pier 4 in the early afternoon. The sun is at its height and I remember why I don't like the beach all that much. Judy looks stunning, though, and she almost skips to the back of the car where we've packed an umbrella, blanket, and a makeshift picnic of cheese and deli meat in leftover grocery store plastic bags. She takes her camera and a bag of chips and leaves me to carry the rest. That's fine by me, though. I like watching her hips sway as we walk up the boardwalk.

It's surprisingly empty and I sit down at a spot in front of the sand dunes where the water won't reach us.

"Let's go down closer," she says. "I can't dip my feet in from way up here."

I take the chips and her camera. "You go on down," I say. "I'll watch you from up here. I'm not feeling like getting wet."

She runs down to the water and I hear her voice carry up the dunes, "It's so warm!"

I sit down on the blanket and watch her for a long time. She dips her whole head in, shooting out of the surf like a rocket. She's spry and has a lot of vigor for someone her age. The two aren't compatible. The woman I see down below me, dancing and playing in the surf, and the woman she'll become after tomorrow. I read a little of my book—some military novel about General Patton—but I can't read for long. My eyes feel heavy and the constant slap of the surf makes me drowsy. I close my eyes for just a second.

The machine is beeping and they're doing another scan and she's puking again only the vomit is bright red and bubbling like tar on a hot sidewalk—like the tar in that building up on 49th when Tim and I spilled a little from the can. She's screaming and the doctors are buzzing like flies around her and prodding and probing and all the while I'm saying this is it this is it but it never is and they send me home with her and she's writhing and crying in our bed in the dark and I'm crying too but I'm trying not to but it's too hard and then tomorrow we go back to the hospital and they do it all again over and over and over and there's too many maybe this' and we'll try's and not enough here we go's and this'll do the trick's and every day is worse until there's a good one and then a bad one follows after and then bad ones ad nauseam and I'm so damn scared all the time and I just want it to end but that's bad because that means she'll end but maybe that's okay because she'll be at peace but will she I don't know I just need to know and something's wet on my face...

Judy's standing over me, spitting water out of

her mouth. It cascades down—right onto my forehead.

"Jeez, Louise!" I shout, confused and disoriented.

She cackles her deep, throaty laugh, water dripping off her chin. "I asked you if you wanted to get in the water!"

I wipe the salt from my eyes. "I didn't hear you."

"You were sleeping!"

"I was just resting," I say, rising to my feet.

"Let's go swi—"

"I'm coming. I'm coming." My feet are sluggish and hot.

The water is warm, and it feels good after the burning sand. She starts splashing me in my eyes so I take her by the shoulders and dunk her under the water. She slides around my body and I pick her out, wet and dripping, and we kiss.

I feel compelled. "I just don't want you to go anywhere," I say.

"Then I won't," she replies.

"I wish it was that simple."

"It is, Ernie. Just trust."

We swim in the sea and bask on the sand until it starts to get dark, then we pack up and walk up the pier to the parking lot. I see her, and a somberness seems to have come over her.

When she notices me looking, she smiles.

"I don't want to tell anyone, alright?"

"What about Chris and Jillian?"

"Especially not them. I don't want them to worry. I just want them to treat me normal. I don't want a bunch of fruit baskets in the mail."

I nod. The only sound is the blinker clicking as we make a left onto the ramp.

"Besides, they'll find out eventually—when the hair goes."

"Maybe it won't."

She laughs, but it's short. "I think it will, Ernie."

"I guess."

"It'll be fine. People beat it all the time." As she says the words I can practically see her going into herself. She puts her hand up to her cheek and lets her head flop over, resting her elbow on the armrest on the door. She's been my wife a long time. I know her better than anyone. I know she's worried, but she's also strong. She's the strongest person I know. If anyone can beat it, it's her. I know it... I hope it.

"We don't have to tell anyone," I say. "We can just keep it between us."

Her voice is choked as the tears stream down, her shoulders heaving. "I just don't want them to see me like that."

I pull the car over and into park and she slumps over against my shoulder. I put my arms around her and hold her tighter than I ever have before, feeling her writhe through the tears. I pull her chin up and say softly, "Hey." Now I'm feeling my own eyes begin to well. "You said so yourself. People beat it all the time. You can do it, Judy."

"I don't know."

"I do. There's hope. You have to hope. As long as there's hope we're going to win. And there's always hope—even if it's just a spark."

"I don't know," she sobs.

Her head resting against my shoulder, my shoulder getting damp, I say, "Me neither."

———————

By the time we find a place to park, it's well after dark. I go to the other side of the car and open the door for her, taking her by the arm. She shambles slowly out. It's like she's become weak already.

I lock the car and together we walk slowly to the apartment—neither saying a word. For me, they'd all fall too flat. Tomorrow is coming and there is nothing we can do about it. People will go about their lives as normal—drinking their coffee and going to their jobs. For the two of us, though. Nothing will ever be normal again.

She mutters "Thanks" as I help her up the stairs of the building. She opens the apartment herself.

"You want some coffee?" I ask, walking to the pot.

She plops down heavily on the chair at the table and holds her head in her hands. "Yeah, that'd be nice."

I make coffee and we sit and sip in the quiet.

The only light is the street bursting in through the window to the side of the television. It casts her pale and white.

After about a half hour, she gets up from the table and walks into the bedroom. "I'm going to shower," she says.

I look and see that she let her coffee go cold. She didn't drink any after all. I hadn't noticed.

I hear the water in the bathroom burst on, filling the apartment with a low drone.

I could sneak a cigarette if I was fast enough. Just run right past when she's done and take a shower to wash the smell off after. But she doesn't like them and that fact weighs heavier now than it usually does.

She walks out in a robe and says with an air of finality, "I'm going to bed."

As she walks away, an electronic chime sounds off loud and strident. The glow of her phone erupts from the counter where she left it.

"Your phone's going," I call out.

She walks slowly out of the bedroom and takes it from the counter. I watch her face in the blue light. It's transforming before my eyes. The creases of her face raise, and a light shines out from her eyes as the smile goes full.

"Oh my God, oh my God!" she squeals, her feet stamping up and down excitedly as her phone shakes in her hand.

"What is it?" I say. I stand up from the table, the chair sliding violently back on the linoleum, and run over to her.

"Look, look, look!" she says, shoving the phone in my face.

I reel back, the screen's too close to see at first. Slowly, it comes into focus. A tiny pink baby wrapped in a white blanket, Jillian cradling it in her arms.

"What! They had the baby?" I shout. I can't contain myself. I run my hand through my hair and look around the room, my smile looking for some face to land on. It lands on Judy's, which grows wider still as she wraps her arms around me and kisses me.

"You're a grandpa...." she says chidingly.

"And you're a grandma, old lady."

She laughs. "I'm so happy. Baby Peter. Maybe if tomorrow goes alright, we could drive down this weekend to see him?"

"Tomorrow will go great."

"Okay," she says. She skips back off to the bedroom, her phone in tow, and closes the door behind her. After a few seconds, she opens it again. "You want to say hi?"

"Nah. You do you. I'll talk to her tomorrow. Tell her I say congrats."

Judy smiles and the door closes in front of her. I hear her dialing and then squeals and laughs and hurried speech as she and Jillian shout and scream and celebrate the new member of the family.

I go to the vase and grab the pack of cigarettes, holding them at my side opposite the door as I walk to the bathroom. I close and lock the door behind me and open the window. The heat and the stink flies through. It won't be gone until September. Outside the sounds of the city have died down to a low roar. I can faintly hear the sound of the bay slapping against the rocks. I'd be able to see it probably if not for the huge brownstone apartment building across the street.

I open the pack and light up a cigarette, making sure the smoke goes out the window. I take a drag and enter a deep calm. Some bird is tweeting. Sounds like a dove. I laugh to myself. I'm feeling strange. Tomorrow begins something new and awful in our lives, and tonight brought something new and wonderful. Peter. It's a beautiful name for a beautiful baby boy.

I lean over the sill and ash down onto the street. No one is around. When I look back up I see movement. It's coming from one of the windows in the old brownstone apartment building. It's a shuffling of whites and pinks that splatters the black of the darkened window—once, twice, three times. I take another drag, the orange glow in front of my face, and I realize to my horror that it's a woman. A bloody woman. Her hair is streaked with pink and red and each pound leaves a bloodier handprint. She's pounding the window—pounding for someone. She needs help. She needs me to help her. Her face cries out in pain.

I toss the smoke down and climb back inside. "Judy, Judy, call the police!" I shout.

Her laughter dies and turns into panic as she bursts out of the bedroom. "Why? What's wrong?"

"Just get them on the phone." I'm running past

her, to the dresser and to the dresser drawer. I open it and grab my revolver. It's loaded. I always keep it loaded.

"Here, here," she says, shoving the phone at me as I pass through. "They're on."

I thrust it up to my ear as I make my way to the front door. The operator on the other line is talking but I shout over her, "Yes, listen. A woman is in trouble. She's in a brownstone apartment building on the corner of 23rd and Garden. The fourth floor, I think, but I'm not sure. She's bleeding. I think she's in a real bad place."

"And where are you now?" the operator asks.

I storm out the door and make my way down the stairs. "I'm going to see if I can help."

"That's no—"

"Just send the cops, alright?" I say, hanging up. I don't need to answer her dumb questions. She just needs to get someone over here fast. I slide the phone into my pocket.

By the time I reach the bottom of the stairs I'm feeling winded and my heart is threatening to jump out of my chest. I slacken my pace a little, but only a little as I cross the street—my eyes firmly fixed on the fourth floor of the building, looking for any sign of the woman. All the windows are dark.

I try the door to the building, but it's locked. I pound on it, shouting, screaming. No one answers. Frantically, I collide into it, smashing it with my shoulder, trying my best to break it open.

"Jesus Christ," a wavering voice cries out in an Irish accent. "Hold your horses."

"Ma'am, I need to get in," I say.

"What are you so excited about?" She's still talking through the door.

"Someone is hurt and I need to help them."

"You need to help them? Why you?"

"Just open the door!"

"Calm down. Patience, young man. Patience."

I take a deep breath. "Please, let me in."

There's no answer. I wait a few seconds that seem like lifetimes. I glance up above me towards the window, but I can't see it because of the second story fire escape that's in the way. "Ma'am! I need to—"

"I'M TRYING to get the damn lock!" She shouts. "Give me a second!"

The lock clicks open. I open the door and storm past the woman—tiny, gray hair in a gray shawl. She mutters something after me but I'm already on the stairs, my knees firing in pain with each step. I get to the fourth floor and there're rows upon rows of doors. 4A, 4B, 4C, 4D, 4E...forever.

"Hello! I'm here to help. Where are you?" I shout.

I hear only a faint echo—the sound of my own voice bouncing off the sharp corners and moldings. Then, there's a tap—more of a scratch. Faint. Barely audible. It's brushing against one of the doors.

I shout, louder than before, "Hello! I'm here to help. You have to tell me where you are!"

The brushing increases, accompanied by the voice of a young woman. It's faint, whimpering...fading. "Here."

"I need you to speak up." I'm scanning the doors, trying to pinpoint where the sound is coming from.

Her voice rings out louder, "I'm here."

I've got it. It's room 4B. I pound on the door, and try the handle. It's locked. "Are you in there?"

"Yes," she says, but quieter than before.

"Stay with me. Can you open the door?"

She doesn't answer.

"Miss, you've got to open the door. I can't come in. It's locked."

Silence.

"You have to let me in. I'm trying to help you, but you've got to let me in."

...

...

"Miss?"

...

...

...

...

...

...

...

...

...

...

...

...

...

...

...

...

...

"Miss!"

...

...

...

...

The click of the lock.

I must be dead because all I see is white. It's blinding, so I close my eyes to shield myself. They don't close. They're just sitting there—the lids fluttering above and below. They're so dry.

I hear voices, but it's like they're underwater. I can't move my head either.

Benjamin's alright now, I guess. He grew up to be a young man and he's got a girlfriend now. She's pretty and cute and polite. I don't know what she sees in Benjy.

He's doing pretty well for himself, he tells me. He's gotten straight B's in all his classes—not the best, but not the worst—and he's working part-time at a bookstore when he's not in class. He even likes books and he's working on one himself! It's called *Hard Times in a Small Town* is a work of genius, a literary achievement crafted by a unique and intelligent voice that truly...

Dad's here now. He's sitting on the side of the bed, his moustache upturned at the ends like it always is when he smiles. He's holding my hand and it's warm, his fingers wrapping around and caressing my palm.

"I thought you were dead," I say.

He laughs and it's a deep, rolling laugh. Deeper than I remember. Too deep. It's almost a growl. It is a growl. It's a grinding growl that sounds like something heavy being dragged across gravel. His skin peels back.

— — — — — — — —

Jim's laying in the bed with me and I'm against his chest. He tells me I don't have to worry anymore because he's here now. I still worry.

— — — — — — — —

"I think we might have something."

— — — — — — —

It's peas and carrots again. It's always peas and carrots because Mom got them from Mrs. Harriet and Mrs. Harriet had a really good year. It's been peas and carrots for weeks.

I don't complain. I just sit there and stare at them, hoping that they'll eventually get tired of looking at me and send me back to my room. Jeffrey's in his high chair cooing and having a great time. He doesn't seem to mind peas and carrots, but he doesn't seem to be eating them either. They're all mushed about his face and hands.

"Oh, please, Jeffy," Mom sighs, wiping his face with her napkin.

"He's just having fun," Dad says, barely looking up from his plate.

"He's making a mess is what he's doing."

"Nah, he's just having fun, aren't you, Jeff?"

Jeffrey puts down his tiny plastic spoon and grasps his hands bashfully as he looks at Dad. He laughs a little, but his eyes fall to Mom, who's scowling at him, and his laughter fades away. I don't know where Benjy is.

"C'mon, Jeffy," she says, scooping up the green mush and attempting to shove it into his mouth.

"You might have to work on your daughter next," Dad says, eyeing my untouched plate. I give him a dirty look.

"Marie," she says to me.

"I'm not hungry," I say. And I'm not. Jessica and I got pizza a few hours ago.

"You have to set a good example for your brother."

I'm a great example.

When dinner's over I go back upstairs and plop down on my bed. I can hear Mom and Dad moving around downstairs, the kitchen sink running, the dishes being dunked in. They'll probably sit there all night in the soapy water until Mom opens the cupboard tomorrow and finds that we have none. Then she'll pour herself a drink and spend the better part of an hour doing them all. Depending on how much she pours herself, she might start on the upstairs bathroom or vacuum the living room rug next. I've had alcohol a few times with Jessica and Rob. It makes your head feel funny and then everything's funny and then you get sleepy. It's a lot of fun.

Rob's not that fun, though. Jessica's all pissed

at him because he stuffed his hands down her pants last weekend at the basketball game. I told her she shouldn't have gone into the bathroom with him, especially considering how horny he always gets, but she did anyway. He told me once that, if he wasn't with Jessica, he'd want to do me. I think about that a lot. He's a real jerk.

I hear Dad climb up the stairs. He's going to bed. He works early, and he always starts nodding off right after dinner. The door to their bedroom closes and I feel more at ease. I hear Mom downstairs talking to Jeffrey.

"Right, and what does a puppy say?"

I don't hear his reply. I'm not sure if he knows yet.

I reach behind me, underneath my pillow, and pull out my bright blue notebook. I read the cover.

FOR MARIE ONLY

I like to write stories. My newest one is about a girl and her puppy who get lost in the woods. Her brother's there too, but they can't find him because he wanders off. I'm at the part where the brother wanders off because he wants to look at these shiny yellow rocks on a hill that's faraway. He thinks that they're gold, but they're really fool's gold. He's a fool.

Dad likes to read my stories, but I hate it when he reads them aloud. I always make him promise not to, but he always ends up doing it anyway. Especially when there are love scenes. He always makes kissing noises when he reads what they're saying. I like it when he reads my stories, though.

I can only write a few sentences before I get tired—just ideas. Eventually I'll type them out on Dad's computer downstairs in his office. I wonder what I'll call it, and I imagine it lined up with all the other stories I've typed out. My favorite is probably this new one I'm doing now. Dad's is "Destructo Daddy" about a dad that becomes part lawn mower.

I carefully tuck the book back under my pillow and lay my head down to see how comfortable it is. I can feel it underneath the pillow alright, but I don't want to move it because one night while I was sleeping Mom stole it out from under the bed when I used to keep it there. I caught her reading it by the nightlight out in the hall and I yelled at her until she gave it back to me. I bet Jessica will try to read my new story. She can be so nosy.

"Mom," I yell from the bed. I wait.

She doesn't answer, but I can still hear her playing with Jeffrey.

"Mom!" I shout, a lot louder than last time.

"What do you want, Marie?" she shouts back.

"Can I call Jessica?"

"You just called her before dinner."

"Yeah, but I want to call her again."

I can hear Mom talking, but her voice sounds all mumbled.

"What?" I yell.

"Make it quick!"

I dial the number but almost as soon as she says hello I lose interest in talking. She moves from talking about Rob and the gross things they do and starts worrying about the Math test we have on Friday. I'm not worried about it. It's not till Friday.

While she talks, I think about what the girl will say to her brother when she finds him.

Jeffrey says Flameo killed Benjy and I want to let him believe it but I don't think he really does. He's too old to really think that. I think he's just playing because he's seen in books how dragons like his little plastic Flameo fly over towns and burn people up. That's what happened to Benjy so it makes sense to him. A lot more sense than his sister was smoking in her room and passed out from a fifth of bourbon.

The pills Dr. Braxton gave me make me feel strange, but I guess they're working. I don't feel sad—just strange.

Mom's dumped out the whole bottle, sliding them over the counter and making a new pile. She doesn't believe me.

"One, two, three, four…"

"You're not crazy, Marie. You're just having a hard time right now is all."

"I think she's coming out. Look at her eyes."

"Give your mother some space."

I'm crying. "But she hasn't said a word to me this whole time. Not since the funeral."

"Everybody grieves differently."

Mom's here—sitting on my bed with Dad. His skin is still off. I thought he went away. I guess he came back but he forgot his skin.

"Did you mean what you said?" I ask her. "That you want me to come home? That you've wanted me to this whole time?"

She doesn't answer, but she's smiling at least.

Dad died, I remember.

There's the white light again, but it's shimmering because my eyes are so wet. I can't stop crying.

"She's here. She's awake," someone says—a

woman dressed all in blue.

"No fucking way," I hear a man say. He's young and his voice is choked with emotion. I feel him take my hand. "Marie, are you in there? For real?"

All I can do is blink, but I guess that's enough because when I do he shakes my hand violently in excitement. "Jesus, I thought you were a goner!"

I feel my head lifted, and it brushes against the short whiskers against his cheek. I still can't make out his face. He hasn't come into view.

"Can I step in a minute?" an older man's voice chimes in, and the younger one backs away. I can tell who the younger one is now. He has the same face.

"Jeffrey," I say, but my lips don't move.

"Conserve your strength, Marie," the older man says. He's dressed in white. "It's going to be baby steps. Nerves take a long time to heal. Don't try to do it all at once." I can see him now, too. My eyes are clear and I can see he's a doctor—the lab coat, the pad—and I'm in a hospital. The smell, how did I not notice it before?

"I'm right here, okay?" Jeffrey says. He's standing against the wall. I can barely see him, but his face is red with emotion, his hand covering his quivering mouth. "I'm right here."

There's a woman with him. Older—maybe in her fifties. Frail, leaning heavily on his arm. The doctors buzz around me as she walks casually over and bends down. It's her. I don't know how, but it is. It's Mom. She bends down and her lips brush against my forehead.

She speaks softly, "It's over now. Home's come to you this time."

"I don't know why I ran—why I was away for so long," I say, the tears streaming down. "I thought you hated me. Why don't you hate me?"

Of course no words come out, my lips don't even move. There's only her smile.

More by
NATE GUTMAN:

BILL THE FLY

PHANTOM SPACE FUNHOUSE (PODCAST)

www.ingramcontent.com/pod-product-compliance
Lightning Source LLC
Chambersburg PA
CBHW060140130626
46556CB00006B/2430